"I need you to tell me where Tyler is."

Carli's body stiffened. "I can't believe you have the nerve to ask me about my brother. His name shouldn't even come out of your mouth after what you put him through. He didn't do this. He didn't kill Sadie."

"The body is on his property. He's the last one who saw her the night she went missing. How could you think I wouldn't ask you that?"

"There's no sense in blaming my brother again. Didn't you and your little Crystal Creek branch of the sheriff's department learn your lesson last time?"

"Then help me. Do what's right and tell me where he is."

Carli turned the key still in the ignition of her Jeep and the engine roared to life. "When you need my statement, I'll be at home."

Carli's phone chimed again. She lifted the device and read the screen. Her face paled.

"What's wrong?"

She flashed the screen in Zain's direction. A text message with an unknown number was displayed.

Sadie's dead. Now I'm coming for you.

Shannon Redmon remembers the first book she checked out from the neighborhood bookmobile, sparking her love of stories. She hopes to immerse readers into a world of faith, hope and love, all from the beautiful scenery of her North Carolina mountain home, where she lives with her amazing husband, two boys and white foo-foo dog named Sophie. Connect with Shannon on Twitter, @shannon_redmon, or visit her online at www.shannonredmon.com.

Books by Shannon Redmon

Love Inspired Suspense

Cave of Secrets

Visit the Author Profile page at Harlequin.com.

CAVE OF SECRETS

SHANNON REDMON

LOVE INSPIRED SUSPENSE
INSPIRATIONAL ROMANCE

LOVE INSPIRED® SUSPENSE
INSPIRATIONAL ROMANCE

ISBN-13: 978-1-335-72202-7

Cave of Secrets

Copyright © 2020 by Shannon Moore Redmon

This edition published by arrangement with Harlequin Books S.A.

For questions and comments about the quality of this book, please contact us
at CustomerService@Harlequin.com.

Love Inspired
22 Adelaide St. West, 40th Floor
Toronto, Ontario M5H 4E3, Canada
www.Harlequin.com

Printed in U.S.A.

Therefore if any man be in Christ,
he is a new creature: old things are passed away;
behold, all things are become new.
–2 Corinthians 5:17

This book is dedicated to my sweet father, Don Moore, who passed away in 2018 from brain cancer. He always inspired me to love God, my amazing family and follow my dreams with all my heart. This one's for you, Daddy.

Also, to all my family and friends who have supported me through this journey, I love you.

ONE

Carli Moore stared at the pile of rocks inside the cave and shivered away the damp feeling of dread building within her. The last time she visited the cavern on her family's ranch was two years ago, before her best friend, Sadie, disappeared.

Volunteers from the small town of Crystal Creek, North Carolina, had scoured every inch of acreage nearby for the twenty-two-year-old beauty, including a thorough combing of Carli's property.

But Sadie's body was never found.

The cave, empty.

Now here Carli stood, moisture from the stone ceiling dripping on her head. She stared at the pile of rocks stretching about five and a half feet long. The same height as her best friend. A swatch of pink poked up from a space between the stones.

The garment was knitted, dirty.

Familiar.

Pressure from her five-year-old nephew's hand patted her leg. "I'm so sorry, Aunt Carli. I didn't mean to run off. I was excited about playing in the cave today."

She'd told Eli about the hideout after her brother left on his business trip. She wanted the boy to experience the same quiet shelter that offered a welcome reprieve from pop-up thunderstorms and southern heat waves like she did as a child.

Now she was rethinking that decision.

Carli forced a smile to her face. "It's okay, bud. I'm glad you yelled for me. Your father and I used to play in here all the time when I was your age. You didn't touch the rocks, did you?"

"Nope." Eli's gaze lifted to hers. "What is it, Aunt Carli?"

She had to spare him from the possibilities coursing through her mind, the dark ideas that took innocent lives from her. She'd never return to this one-red-light town if Eli and her brother, Tyler, didn't live here.

She lifted the boy into her arms and carried him to the other side of the cave, then handed Eli her battery-powered lantern.

"Probably an animal. Let me take a closer look. You hold the light for me, okay?"

Red curls bobbed on top of his head as he accepted his task. She couldn't resist tousling the cuteness with her fingers before returning to the revelation awaiting her.

Carli scanned every superficial detail, but no other clues to what was underneath presented themselves. She knelt onto the cavern floor. Moisture seeped through the fabric of her riding pants and her fingers shook as she reached out, knocking a couple of stones away. Their clamor a soundtrack to the horror unfolding before her.

A human skeleton.

Dirty blond hair still attached to the scalp.

Nothing but bones left elsewhere.

Every muscle in Carli's body tensed and she fell backward. Eli ran toward her. She pushed to her feet and grabbed him, clamping a hand over the boy's eyes and pulling him to her side.

"Come on, bud."

"Can I see?"

"No." She spat out a little too harshly. "Let's go get someone to help clean up."

She lifted her nephew and held his head against her shoulder, the lantern still swinging in his small hand.

Light brushed across a heart-shaped wall carving, framing a pair of initials. Carli tried to ignore the marks as they exited the smaller room. She had loved Zain Wescott at one time, but that was a few years ago. A time when her parents were still alive and Sadie was still her best friend.

Right now, her main focus was to protect Eli from the ever-present realization creeping into her brain.

Sadie was dead.

Unless she was wrong, which wouldn't be the first time. They'd searched this cave before and found nothing. Could a body remain intact this long, after two years had passed? And if so, how did Sadie get here?

Maybe the body belonged to someone else. Another missing person Carli didn't even know. Still a sad situation, but she could hold on to hope Sadie was still alive, somewhere on a faraway beach, living her best life. There were plenty of missing girls with blond hair and pink sweaters.

Carli swiped away a tear. If only she could convince the gnawing in her gut the same thing.

The clop of a horse's hooves stamped with impatience near the main opening of the cave. Cocoa, her favorite horse, expressed displeasure at being tied up. Carli lifted Eli into the saddle, mounted behind him and gave Cocoa a pat. "You get to gallop this time, boy."

The black Arabian chomped at the bit to run and took off at the click of his owner's tongue. What were her next steps?

Zain needed to know.

He was Sadie's brother and sergeant of criminal investigations for the Henderson County sheriff's department. His team would investigate no matter the identity of the body.

She hadn't seen him since she left two years ago, having chosen to leave Crystal Creek without a proper goodbye. When she did visit for holidays and special family occasions, she kept her distance from town. The people she'd grown up with weren't too kind when her brother was accused of murdering her best friend.

"Where we going, Aunt Carli?"

"Sergeant Wescott's house. He always eats lunch at home and he's the closest neighbor we have."

She wrapped an arm tight around her nephew and steered the horse toward Zain's road.

Maybe she should wait for the medical examiner's autopsy before drawing any conclusions about the body's identity and opening old wounds. That would be the wise thing to do. The body *could* be someone else.

She still had to tell Zain.

If only she could trust him not to come after her brother again. Tyler was the last person to see Sadie alive and this became the foundation of the sheriff's department's case, but with no other evidence found, Tyler was released without charges. Didn't matter.The townspeople had already convicted him…and her. They all gossiped about her drunken state the night of Sadie's disappearance. Carli had talked her best friend into going to the Summer's End party. It was her fault that Sadie was dead and this town would never let her forget.

At least life for Tyler had finally calmed down over the past year and her brother had made a good life for himself and Eli. The ranch business was booming from customers across the country wanting his well-bred horses, like the one she rode now.

Cocoa rounded the bend onto the Wescotts' long gravel drive. Zain's farmhouse came into view, across a pretty wooden bridge covering Crystal Creek. She slowed Cocoa to a trot, his horse's hooves clamoring on the wooden slats. A wisp of coolness arose from the waters beneath.

She tugged on the reins and slowed her horse to a stop.

Hinges on the front screen door creaked their disapproval when Zain stepped from his two-story home, sky blue eyes fixed on hers and a curious expression on his face. The lines in his forehead deepened with her intrusion. Not exactly how she planned to reunite after all these years.

His toned arms folded across the chest of his uniform as he leaned against the post, and a gentle breeze blew the waves of his dark hair. A bit longer than she remembered. He was always hard to resist in his uniform, but time and hurt had faded the temptation.

Sunlight gleamed off his sergeant's badge. A recent promotion according to her brother. He'd been a deputy in the police department when they dated. Now, he was twenty-eight years old, four years her senior, and being groomed for a promotion when Lieutenant Black retired.

How was she supposed to tell him about his sister's body buried in the cave? The news would destroy any hope of finding Sadie alive. A hope unfaded even as the seasons passed.

Carli leaned toward Eli's car. "Hey, bud. Why don't you go play on the tire swing? I need to talk to Sergeant Wescott for a minute."

Her nephew slid from the saddle and skipped over to the large oak tree. Carli dismounted and forced her weakened legs to approach the bottom porch step, while shoving her hands into her back jean pockets to hide their trembles.

Zain's gaze never left her face. "Long time since you've been to my place."

Waves of regret and pain rolled through her. "I need to talk to you."

He probably wouldn't believe her. Most people in town counted her a liar, a sister protecting her brother's life.

"We haven't talked in two years, Carli. You ran off to Atlanta and never looked back. What could you possibly have to say to me now?"

If only he knew how many times she'd wanted to talk to him, or dreamed of walking in open pastures by his side. Many lonely nights she pulled up his phone number, letting her thumb hover over his name, then swiped it away for lack of words. A justified silence out of respect for Sadie…at least that's what she told herself, until now.

"I found a body. I think it might be her."

He straightened at her announcement, the words tightening his facial muscles. "You mean Sadie?"

She nodded.

"We've searched this entire county three times over for my sister. Why do you think a body you found is hers?"

Carli flashed a quick look at Eli, laughing as the tire swing twirled him in circles. So innocent. What she wouldn't give to return to those days. Her eyes lifted back to Zain's.

"Because the pink sweater covering the corpse I found…is mine."

The rumors were true. Carli Moore was back in town and stood only a few feet from Zain.

Just like the good ole days.

Almost as if nothing had changed. That the past two years of absence and his sister's disappearance hadn't destroyed their relationship.

Carli's beauty struck his heart with a familiar ache. Seeing her now replaced his daily memories with the real, updated version. Kind eyes, green, framed with long black lashes, and full lips pressed together.

Suppressed issues, never discussed, filled the space between them, trumped by Carli's discovery of a dead body. After all this time, she returned claiming she had found Sadie's corpse.

Zain had buried any hope of ever finding his sister when the case closed, unsolved. He wasn't ready to reopen old wounds, but Carli had a way of stirring up their troubled past.

"A lot of girls wear pink sweaters," he said, relying on years of learned discernment with the sheriff's department.

Logical thinking was key, despite the turmoil fermenting inside him. Emotions only clouded a person's judgment. He had to be objective and differentiate truth from false information. Most witness accounts were greedy people trying to capture reward money anyway.

But not Carli. She didn't need any extra cash. Their thriving family ranch, managed by her brother, Tyler, plus four ranch hands and one nanny named Marta, brought in a substantial wealth for them both.

Most of Tyler's customer base came from out of town, not from the people who lived in Crystal Creek. Carli's savvy marketing skills helped her brother build a huge internet following. People from all over the world purchased his horses.

Plus, she collected a substantial salary from her high-paying marketing job in Atlanta, another reason their relationship ended. She chose her career and money over him, while he struggled to provide for his sick mother who grieved each day for his sister.

If only Carli had been responsible the night of the late summer party instead of drinking, then his life might be different. Sadie was the smart one in the family. A nurse manager at Dr. Candyce Frye's office. She'd planned to go back to school and get her practitioner license. But then she disappeared. Life over in a matter of minutes.

Carli brushed a strand of hair from her face. The noonday sun augmented the red highlights. "I dropped my pink sweater on the way to the car. Somewhere near the barn. Sadie went back to get it for me. That was the last time I saw her."

"I'm surprised you remember."

He regretted the words as soon as they tumbled out. Carli dropped her gaze and dug the gravel with her boot heel. Up until now, she'd been unable to remember any details to help with his sister's case, a by-product of regretful intoxication.

Not that it was all her fault. He should've done a better job too. The one thing they still had in common—blame and guilt for not protecting Sadie when either of them had a chance.

Carli's green eyes lifted back to his, the pain of his statement reflecting in their depths. Trying to apologize now would make the moment more awkward.

"Wait here."

Zain reentered the cool of his home, grabbed his gun and keys from the table by the front door and exited again. He descended the porch stairs, his black boots hitting the gravel where she stood. "Where's this body at?"

She averted her gaze from his. "In the cave, under a pile of rocks. Smaller room off to the left."

Zain crossed the yard in three strides and jumped in his new SUV. He rolled down the window, allowing heat to escape. "You comin'?"

"Let me drop off Eli with Marta. I'll meet you there."

"Fine."

He started the engine, shifted into gear and pressed the gas pedal, leaving dust swirling in his rearview mirror. Carli grew smaller with the distance. At least she was the one watching his taillights fade this time.

Things might've been different if she'd returned his phone calls or answered some of his texts after she left. They could've healed together, but silence was the only answer he ever received. How does someone leave a love like they had? There was only one answer, she didn't love him as much as he loved her.

Gravel crunched beneath his tires as he sped down the road, fresh air whipping around him. The radio played a sad country song. He punched the knob and cut the noise. Not really in the mood for music.

The cave was up ahead. He'd have to cross the field at the first bend to get to the entrance. A place he knew well.

Most of his childhood and teenage memories had Carli and the Moore family ranch in them. Not a day went by they didn't have some adventure together, like making a rope swing and dropping into the refreshing creek behind their houses or conducting paint gun wars in the open fields and old buildings.

The cave was where they all hung out when they needed a cool place to rest, eating snacks and discussing important life events, like the newest video games to play.

His best memories came from the Moore family's annual New Year's Eve bash thrown for the entire town. Best fireworks show ever. Zain's first real kiss with Carli was there, on top of the barn roof, with an array of colors bursting over their heads, a year and a half before his sister disappeared. All those celebrations stopped after Carli's parents and her sister-in-law died in a crash on the Blue Ridge Parkway. She was devastated at losing them.

Maybe that's why her departure felt like a huge betrayal. Of all the people in town, Carli was the one person who understood his pain from losing a loved one. He needed her more than he realized, and her departure was a loss second only to the disappearance of his sister.

A large rock face rose up from the field. Zain cut off the road and bounced through the humps and divots of the pasture, then pulled to the cave's front entrance. He stared at the opening, a rush of adrenaline increasing his heart rate.

Before today, the shady entrance was a welcome sight for someone looking for shelter, but the gray slate loomed like a giant tombstone above him.

What if Sadie *was* inside?

Zain exited his truck and entered the cavern. The glow of his flashlight bounced against the walls. He donned a pair of plastic gloves, then headed to the smaller room off the main cave.

The rocks Carli described were piled in the corner, a swatch of pink fabric visible.

He inched his way closer. A cold dread numbed his usual heightened impulses triggered by a crime scene. Not like he hadn't seen a dead body before. But this one was likely his sister. Everything in him rebelled against the possibility.

He knelt down and touched the sweater. The same one with the chipped plastic button Carli wore the night of the party. Most people thought redheads shouldn't wear pink, but not Carli. She loved the color and wasn't going to let other's impressions guide her decisions.

Zain pushed away the rest of the stones.

Tears burned the corners of his eyes and pain stabbed across his forehead. Sadie's dirty blond hair blurred against the backdrop of gray. Her favorite butterfly hair clip still clasped in the strands. He pressed the palms of his hands to his eyes in an effort to hold off the onslaught of anguish.

"Zain?"

He stood, his back to Carli, and swiped the wetness from his cheeks. "Yeah?"

If anyone understood his pain, she did, but crying showed weakness. Not acceptable for a sergeant who must deny any emotional attachment during a case. Everything by the book. No more mistakes.

He turned and faced her. "I didn't hear you come in."

Carli stepped closer, her eyes locking with his. "It's her, isn't it?"

"Most likely."

Before he could say any more, Carli pressed into his arms, wrapping her body against his, head to his chest, dampening his shirt with her sobs. He held her there, letting the common denominator of grief wash away all the betrayal from their past. At least for the moment.

He didn't want to let her go, but he had a job to do. "I've got to call my team. We need to gather evidence."

"Of course." She stepped away, wiping her face. "I'll head back to the house."

"Actually, I'm going to need you to stick around for a while. Provide an official statement."

"Sure. I'll wait in my Jeep. Let me know when you're ready."

Zain remained by the cave entrance until she was in her vehicle, then he called Detective Nate Steele, one of his forensics service team members and former partner. "I'm going to need a team at the Moore family ranch."

Computer keys clicked in the background

along with the typical hum of an office setting. Nate was most likely completing several reports he failed to turn into Zain last week.

"What for?"

His colleague had a bad habit of questioning everything. Of course, that's what made him a good detective, but today, Zain struggled to provide the answer.

"A body's been found in a cave located on the property." He swallowed. "I think…it's Sadie's and if the medical examiner agrees, I'm going to need you to take the lead on this. Lieutenant Black will want someone other than the brother of the deceased overseeing this case."

Zain paused for a moment and ran a hand over the back of his neck. "Do you remember who our key suspect is?"

Silence on the other end resonated through the call. No more key clicks. He had Nate's full attention now. "Yeah, Tyler Moore."

Zain gripped the phone tighter in his hand. The evidence had been circumstantial last go around and without a body, the man walked. Zain was convinced Tyler killed his sister. He was the last one to see her and everyone else in the vicinity had a solid alibi. Tyler didn't.

Zain would prove his case this time.

"Exactly. This is what we've been waiting for.

He messed up and my sister's body is on his property. Time to bring this guy to justice."

"What about Carli? She caused a lot of problems with our investigation last time."

Zain glanced back at his former girlfriend. She sat inside her air-conditioned Jeep, head resting back against the seat, eyes closed. Every few seconds she swiped tears from her face.

The defense lawyer she hired for her brother the first time was a real barracuda. Some hotshot out of Atlanta. The district attorney dropped the case after one meeting with the man and never charged Tyler with a crime. Then Carli left. Moved away from Zain for good. He couldn't let his past feelings interfere with the job he had to do.

"I'm hoping she'll be cooperative."

"And if she isn't?"

He straightened and glanced back toward the tomb of his sister. "We follow the letter of the law. No shortcuts or favors. Gather all the evidence. We're not messing this up again."

"Got it."

Zain ended the call and approached Carli's Jeep. She didn't see him as she typed on her phone. Tyler's name displayed at the top of her screen.

Already alerting her brother to their discovery. Word around town was the man left for a while. Some said his departure was work related, others said he went to meet a girl, but who really knew. Gossip ran rampant in Small Town, USA.

Zain tapped her window. Her body startled at the noise and she flipped over her device, placing it on the console, then lowered the glass. "Are they on their way?"

"Medical examiner's office is in Hendersonville. He should be here in about fifteen minutes. The dental records will provide a positive identification. We should know pretty soon if the body is Sadie's."

Her gaze shifted to the fields in front of her. "You and I both know it is."

He wasn't ready to agree until he had an official report. Other murders had happened in the area since his sister's disappearance, and he would wait until evidence confirmed the finding.

"The rest of my team will be here in five to collect evidence."

Her phone vibrated once, but she ignored the message and white-knuckled the steering wheel. "I can't get the sight of her out of my mind. How do you think she got there? We searched the cave several times the weeks following her disappearance. No one ever found her body."

"I think someone moved her, and if this is Sadie, there's one thing I'm going to need from you."

Her eyes flashed to his. "Sure. Anything."

"I need you to tell me where Tyler is."

Her body stiffened and she averted her gaze back to the field. "I can't believe you have the nerve to ask me about my brother. His name shouldn't even come out of your mouth after what you put him through. He didn't do this. He didn't kill Sadie."

"The body is on his property. He's the last one who saw her the night she went missing. How could you think I wouldn't ask you that?"

"There's no sense in blaming my brother again. Didn't you and your little Crystal Creek branch of the sheriff's department learn their lesson last time? Don't start up this nightmare again."

"Then help me. Do what's right and tell me where he is."

Carli shifted the gear into Drive. "When you need my statement, I'll be at home."

Her phone chimed again. She lifted the device and read the screen. Her face paled.

"What's wrong?"

She flashed the screen in his direction. A text message with an unknown number displayed.

Sadie's dead. Now I'm coming for you.

TWO

Carli stared at the screen.

She had started receiving scary texts two years ago when her brother was a suspect. Nothing ever came of them. Just empty threats. Some mean-spirited townie trying to put fear into her day, but God did not give Carli a spirit of fear. She chose to ignore the texts, but this one seemed different.

"How do they know Sadie's dead? Your team's not even here yet to process the scene."

Zain glanced at the landscape around her and she followed his gaze.

Open pastureland surrounded them with the old barn in the distance. Crystal Creek meandered at the rear of the building, along the edge of their property. The new barn Tyler built six months ago sat about a hundred yards away from the other structure. Horses grazed in the fields and Cocoa trotted around his favorite mare.

Zain tapped his hands on the driver door. "I

don't know, unless this text is from the person who killed Sadie."

"Then that should be enough for you to realize my brother is innocent."

He eyed her for a moment and then cut his gaze back toward the cave. "I'll take that into consideration."

"So glad you're willing to consider that my brother would never threaten his own sister."

Carli pressed the gas and dust swirled as she pulled onto the gravel road leading back toward the family's home.

Zain infuriated her.

He had a one-track mind and was determined to blame everything on Tyler. Time to call the same lawyer who helped them the first time Tyler was questioned. Carli left the man a message and made one more phone call to Marta, her nanny. The older woman picked up in her usual happy singsong voice.

"I'm heading out for a drive to clear my head. Can you keep an eye on Eli for me?"

"Sure, honey. But have you seen all the police cars on our property?"

She was hoping Marta would be busy and not notice all the law enforcement descending on their place. "Yeah. I called them. We think we found Sadie's body."

"Oh, honey. Why don't you come home? I'll

make you some hot tea. You don't need to be alone right now."

"Thanks, but this is something I have to do."

"Where are you going?"

Carli was hoping she wouldn't ask. "Bad Fork Overlook."

"Oh, Carli. Why are you going there today? After you found Sadie? This is not good for you to be alone at the place where your parents died."

"I feel close to them there." She knew it sounded morbid, but somehow visiting their last location brought her comfort, and after finding her best friend's body, plus dealing with her emotions for Zain, she needed to be alone. "I won't stay long."

She ended the call, cutting off Marta's protest, and wound up on the Blue Ridge Parkway. Rain dotted her windshield and oncoming headlights broke through the dusky sky. If she didn't hurry, then the view would be clothed in darkness.

The Bad Fork Overlook was true to its name, and the sharp curve leading to the parking area was deemed the main culprit in her parents' accident. An overcorrection on her father's part, with a plunge down the steep mountainside, took three of the most important people from her life.

Carli questioned the conclusions of the accident report. Police details didn't add up and she believed there was foul play.

Milepost 399 opened on her right and she parked, stepping from her vehicle. White fog drenched the layers of mountains in a mist of rain, drizzling on her head. Not enough to soak her, but still she grabbed her green jacket from the back seat and pulled up the hood.

A rock border edged the parking area, and she stepped on top. Carli forced herself to look down even though high places terrified her. A deep chasm dropped below. The tops of evergreen trees hid the steep decline to the rocky bottom.

The increased elevation triggered dizziness, and trees spun around her. She stepped away from the edge as the rain increased.

She ran back to her Jeep, climbed inside and lowered her hood. The storm had moved in quick and rain pelted the scene on the other side of the windshield. She left the engine off and listened to the water pound the metal roof.

Her parents were gone. Eli's mom too. All taken without any warning.

Now Sadie was dead.

Maybe she should pack up Eli and Marta for a visit to Atlanta. Get out of town for a few days. Tyler would understand.

Her cell phone buzzed.

"Hello?"

"I thought you told me to come by your house to get your statement."

Zain.

"I did."

"Then why weren't you at home when I stopped by?"

"I had to take a drive. Clear my head. I figured of all people you'd understand that."

"I do."

A tap clanked her passenger window. Zain stood outside her door, rain rushing over his body like a monsoon. The sight of him washed a bit of elation through her. Why did seeing him always stir up so many emotions?

Carli hit the unlock button and he climbed into her Jeep and tossed his hat into the back seat.

"What are you doing here?" she asked.

"Marta told me where to find you. The woman worries…a lot."

"I don't know why. I'm a grown woman. I come and go as I please when I'm in Atlanta. She never sends a babysitter after me there."

"She cares about you and knows how the parkway is not a place for a woman to be at night. If you knew all the crimes that happen up here, you'd never come back."

"Like the death of my mom and dad."

Zain paused and ran a hand through his dark wet hair. "Yeah. Like that."

They hadn't been this close in years, especially not in the same car. He still wore the same spicy cologne as when they dated. Although tonight it was a bit more muted and moisture laden. They used to love to take drives on the parkway together, picking out future towns of where they wanted to live. Carli turned her head away from him to dampen down the memories.

"Your current lieutenant was the sergeant on duty the night they died. He told Tyler that crews brought in a crane to recover the car and the bodies. He believed someone else was involved in their deaths, but when the official report was finally released, they ruled the wreck as an accident."

Carli closed her eyes and let the memory play in her mind. Lieutenant Black standing at her door, his announcement of her parents' deaths ripping into her world like a tornado. "Tyler used to come up here and hunt for clues. He was convinced the tire marks plunging over the mountainside had been caused by someone else. Like they'd been pushed over the edge. To this day the facts still don't add up."

"Reports ruled it an accident. Said they swerved to avoid hitting a deer and went over. Makes sense to me."

Gravel crunched behind Carli's Jeep and a black truck parked several spaces down. The windows were tinted and no one exited the vehicle. Not too odd, since some people liked to take in a quick view and then continue along the famous road.

Zain blew into his hands. "I get you want to understand what happened to your parents, the same way I want to know what happened to Sadie, but I don't think we're going to figure it out tonight. Why don't we head back to your house? I'll get the statement and promise to review your parents' case with you. Maybe you'll find it really was an accident."

She stared out the windshield. "I stood out there on the ledge."

Zain shifted in his seat toward her. "You did what?"

"The drop is steep. Almost straight down. I can't imagine the terror they must have felt."

"Carli, I know all this has upset you and I'm devastated too, but putting your life at risk is not going to help."

Her eyes met his. There was no judgment in them. Just concern. Genuine and real, like when he loved her before.

Bright lights glared from the rearview mirror and interrupted the nostalgic moment. The black truck, parked several spaces down, had moved behind them. She hadn't even noticed until now.

They both turned and looked back through the rain-dotted window.

"What is he doing?" Carli asked.

"I don't know, but I think we need to move."

"What about your car?"

"I'll have Nate drive me up tomorrow and get it."

Carli shifted into Reverse and rolled backward.

The truck barged toward them. Iron bars dressed the front grille.

"He's coming right at—"

The impact hit hard and shoved them forward…toward the steep cliff.

Zain unsnapped his gun and rolled down the window. Rain blew in through the opening. The tires spun but the Jeep's brakes were not strong enough to keep them from moving forward. "He's pushing us toward the wall."

"More like trying to push us over."

Carli switched her foot to the gas, and pressed the pedal to the floor. Her tires squealed on the pavement.

Zain popped out of the window and fired three shots, then slid back into the car.

The truck backed off, swerved to the side and lowered the driver-side window. A large-barreled rifle pointed toward the Jeep.

"Go, Carli. Move!"

She shifted into Drive, hit the gas and swerved toward the road. Multiple shots whizzed across the space they vacated.

The truck followed, activating a light bar to blind their vision through the mirrors.

Zain pressed the key on his radio. "Dispatch, C50, black pickup truck on Blue Ridge Parkway headed north toward Highway 276. Multiple shots fired at our vehicle, blue Jeep Wrangler. Send backup. I repeat, send backup."

Carli adjusted the reflections out of her eyes. A tunnel emerged up ahead. "Great."

"What?"

"A tunnel."

"Stay in the middle. I'll fire a couple more rounds and keep him off of us."

She accelerated and Zain hoped she was able to get through before the truck caught them again. Bright lights dispersed the darkness in the tunnel and spotlighted their vehicle, like a deer being hunted.

Zain leaned out the window and popped off a few more rounds, then slid back inside. Carli clung to the steering wheel and swerved to the middle of the road.

Another gun fired. Glass exploded from the back window with the hit.

An oncoming car entered the tunnel.

Carli was in the wrong lane, slated for a head-on collision.

She swerved. The passenger door scraped against the stone wall, and Carli steered toward the middle.

Zain admired her quick thinking. She drove better than some of his deputies that had been through defensive driving school. Zain popped his magazine. "I'm out of bullets."

Carli motioned toward the console. "I've got my gun in there. The one you bought me."

"I thought you hated that gun."

"It's not my rifle, but I needed a smaller one when I moved to Atlanta for protection. Got pretty good at shooting. Should be loaded."

He opened the lid and pulled out her revolver.

The truck sped closer. Headlights, larger, brighter, engulfing them in the glare. Zain climbed in the back seat and fired every round. One hit the front bumper.

Another strong impact spun the Jeep three hundred and sixty degrees, outside the tunnel.

Greenery blurred around them. Rocks scraped against metal. So fast, yet slow at the same time. Carli's eyes closed. Zain grabbed the wheel to keep the car from descending off the edge. The Jeep crashed to a halt against the upper side of the mountainous road.

The black truck flew right by, leaving them in a ditch.

Zain's heart raced. Breathing short, rapid. Nothing was broken.

He brushed his fingers against Carli's cheek. "Talk to me. Are you okay?"

"Yeah. A little shaky, but okay."

Zain leaned his head back against the seat and radioed again to dispatch. "Our vehicle crashed. Suspect continued toward Highway 191. Who's close?"

"Officer Steele will be there in three."

Heaviness invaded Zain's body as the adrenaline faded. "Shouldn't be much longer," he said to Carli, placing a hand on her forearm, her skin smooth and warm under his touch. Her fingers pressed against his. Like old times.

Zain made a silent vow to do everything in his power to protect her. Carli's life was in danger and he would die before he let anything happen to her.

THREE

Blue lights flashed off the wet slab of rock mountain moistened by the earlier storm. Zain walked around the outside of Carli's vehicle, inspecting the damage. She was fortunate to be alive. What if he hadn't been with her? Would she be standing beside him, wrapping a strand of red hair around her finger? Probably not.

"Looks like it's totaled," she said.

"You're going to need something else to drive." He clenched his teeth as the reality of the situation hit him. "Perhaps a tank."

She laughed at his joke. Her contagious smile lit up her eyes, a sight he'd missed over the years, but one he'd learned to live without. He kept his tone serious. The last thing he needed was to fall for Carli Moore again. She'd already broken his heart once. "Any idea why someone would want you dead?"

"Everything's been fine until I found Sadie this afternoon."

"And within hours of finding my sister, we were almost shoved off the side of a mountain? Not good."

Nate stepped from his SUV. "You guys okay?"

Zain nodded. "Not sure if *okay* is the best word, but we have no injuries that need medical attention."

Nate grazed the glow of his flashlight over them both. "Looks like you've got a small cut on your head, Carli."

She wiped the spot with her fingers. "It's just a scratch. I'm okay."

"Well, the paramedics and a tow truck are on their way. Tell me what happened again."

Zain relayed the story to him from her stop at the overlook to what brand of vehicle wrecked them with the iron grille on the front.

"Did you say a black Chevy truck with bars?"

"Yeah. You know it?"

"Maybe. We had another similar incident last month. No one was injured, but the car was crushed. We haven't been able to locate the truck yet."

Zain handed him Carli's revolver. "Well, now you have a better identifying mark to help you."

"What?"

"The bullet hole from Carli's .38 Special. I shot the front of the truck."

More blue lights flashed in the darkness and

pulled into another overlook not far from where they stood. Lieutenant Black led the pack. Zain liked working for the man. He was honorable, consistent and always tried to do the right thing.

"Sergeant Wescott, are you all okay?"

"Yes, sir."

"I heard the calls. Scary situation with someone ramming into your car trying to push you over the mountain's edge, Ms. Moore."

Carli raised her chin with determination. Zain had seen that look before. Not a good one. That expression usually preceded arguments they'd had.

"Kind of like the death of my family, don't ya think?" she asked.

Zain stepped up beside her and leaned toward her ear. "Not the time."

She took a step closer toward his lieutenant. "Weren't you the officer who wrote up the report the day my parents and Eli's mother died, Lieutenant?"

"I did. Their deaths were ruled an accident."

"That's not what you thought when you first observed the scene. Tyler told me the details you shared with him. After tonight, seems like the two incidents might be related."

"I doubt it. Our team did a thorough investigation, and the wreck was an accident."

Carli shook her head. "Your statement said

there was foul play. The tire tracks found in the mud didn't match my father's car. Was all the evidence considered back then? And what about tonight? Was this an accident too?"

A growing uneasiness turned inside of Zain. He'd been with Carli the night her family was killed. Nothing prepared a person for the loss of their loved ones. He'd tried to support her, but something changed between them after they were gone.

Seemed like the two years in Atlanta had done little to help her heart heal. The wound was still raw.

He placed a hand on her arm. "Carli, we can set up a meeting at the office to discuss this. Where we can look at the actual reports—"

Lieutenant Black folded his arms across his chest. "It's okay, Zain. I don't mind answering her questions."

The man took a step forward. "Let me assure you, Ms. Moore, I have no idea who rammed into you tonight, but this was clearly not an accident. As for your parents and sister-in-law, I made my thoughts known about the so-called 'foul play' you mentioned to the crime scene investigators. You know what they found?"

Carli swallowed and shook her head.

"They found out, after a thorough investigation of your father's car, that a tuft of deer fur was stuck in the grille. They think your father swerved to avoid hitting the animal and most likely lost control of the car, sending them over the edge. The tire tracks you mentioned were from a bystander and firsthand witness to the events. He was the one who called 911 and reported the accident."

A look of defeat filled Carli's face, exhaustion weighing down her slumped shoulders. Zain needed to get her home.

"No one ever told me about the deer or the witness."

"Every detail is in the final report. Feel free to have Sergeant Wescott email a copy. Now, I'm happy to give you both a ride back to the ranch. The tow truck will take your Jeep to the storage warehouse. We need to have the evidence team go over it with a fine-tooth comb, see if we can figure out who might've tried to kill you tonight."

Zain motioned up the road. "We only need a ride to the overlook. My SUV is parked there. Since Carli's my neighbor, I can drop her by her house on my way home."

Lieutenant Black shot him a warning look. The man had been there through his heartache after Carli left. Zain moved to the vehicle to avoid the uneasiness, opened the back door of the SUV while Carli climbed inside. "I'll get you home, so you can get some sleep."

"Thanks. I need it."

Police lights flashed across her pale skin, making her eyes change to blue.

"Sergeant Wescott. A moment."

Zain glanced over his shoulder at his lieutenant. He didn't look happy, jaw clenched. He knew what was coming. Zain closed the door and turned to face him, glancing at Carli as she watched from the back seat.

"What do you need, sir?"

The man's arms were folded tighter than a banjo string. "You want to tell me why you're the one getting Ms. Moore's statement about your sister's body?"

"She found the body and came and got me, sir. I thought I should get her statement while it was fresh in her mind."

"Was Detective Steele on-site?"

"Yes, sir."

"He's the one in charge of this investigation. In fact, stay away from Sadie's case. Let Nate handle the details. If you don't, I'll have you on desk duty so fast, you won't see the outside of a police car for a very long time. Are we clear?"

Zain nodded and glanced toward Carli again. "Yes, sir."

* * *

Rain pecked on Carli's bedroom window and dim morning light filtered inside dismissing sleep. She wasn't ready to get up, but the alarm on her phone wouldn't stop the annoying chime if she didn't roll over and hit the snooze button.

She groaned as she moved. Her muscles ached from the demolition derby on the parkway last night. Grateful to be alive, she shuddered to think what might have happened had Zain not followed her to the overlook.

He hadn't changed. Always looking out for her, providing for her. Always wanting more than she could give. They'd tried to be a couple and failed. Other people broke up all the time and moved on. Why couldn't she? The last thing she needed was her heart broken again by Zain Wescott. She had a good life in Atlanta and as soon as Tyler returned, she'd go back to it.

Carli rubbed her eyes and sat up in bed, letting her feet dangle above the hardwood floors.

Sadie was gone. For good.

Today, her friend's body was being searched for clues to identify her killer. Another reason to crawl back into bed and not come out for a while.

She fell onto the pillows and pulled her white duvet over her head.

Buzz.

Stupid phone.

She really needed a hammer for the thing. Carli peeked her head out as the device danced across the wood surface. She grabbed it and swiped the screen.

I didn't get you last night, but I won't stop until I do.

Carli sat up and read the text again. Instant shivers caused her fingers to tremble as she tried to delete the message. Another consequence of finding Sadie's body.

After last night's events, the message held more clout. She should show this to Zain, instead of deleting it. He could investigate the source. But if she gave him one glance, he'd go into security mode and put her under surveillance if he hadn't already.

Carli locked her phone, showered and dressed, then headed downstairs. Eli sat in his father's seat at the end of the kitchen table. She ruffled the messy curls on his head and gave him a kiss that he tried to dodge, almost knocking Marta over with his motion.

Carli laughed and glanced out the window. An unmarked cop car sat on the edge of her drive.

"Looks like we have company."

Marta followed her gaze. "That's Deputy Judd. He's been here all night. Came to the door after you went to bed and told me to let him know if we needed anything."

Marta patted Carli's shoulder, then opened the refrigerator door. "How does a southwestern scramble sound for breakfast this morning? I figured we might need something hardy to get us started after everything with Sadie and your ordeal last night."

"Sounds amazing." Carli gave the nanny, who had been her rock for many years, a side hug. Marta offered a slight smile, accentuated by sad, puffy eyes.

The woman was overcome with worry. Marta had heard the wreck on the police scanner she kept by her bed and gave Carli a good scolding after she checked her from head to toe for injuries. Carli didn't mind. It was nice to have someone love her like that.

She popped a fresh piece of bacon into her mouth, then filled her coffee mug with must-have caffeine to get through her day. "Have you heard from Tyler?"

"Not since he called you. When was that? Tuesday?"

"Yeah. He promised he'd keep in touch and knows how panicked I get when I don't hear from him." A trait she acquired when her parents didn't call the night of their tragic accident. She probably owed Lieutenant Black an apology after the grilling she gave him. Maybe a visit to the sheriff's office might not be a bad item to add to her schedule.

Marta cracked a couple of eggs in the pan. "You know what they say, no news is good news."

No news only made Carli's heart worry.

Tyler's last call was four nights ago to talk with Eli. Everything in her world was fine at that point. Now things were falling apart. She needed God's peace more than ever, but her thoughts kept drifting to her brother and the horrible images of Sadie still plastered in her brain. She hoped nothing had happened to him.

"Do you want jalapeños?" Marta asked.

"A few will be fine. Thank you."

At least she had Marta, who stirred eggs into a whipped, fluffy concoction. The woman had been a part of her life for as long as Carli could remember. Marta came to live with their family right after Carli was born. She'd never known a day without her sweet friend.

After her parents died, Marta filled a lonely void and kept their family moving forward. Plus, she cooked better than anyone in town.

Carli drained her mug empty. For some reason, coffee always helped her wake up. She needed alertness right now, a clear mind.

She rose and poured more of the dark liquid into her cup, then added vanilla creamer.

Zain used to make fun of her for her blond drink before they split up. He'd been super quiet on the ride back to the ranch last night. Probably wishing she'd never come back to town. Seemed like when she was in Crystal Creek, she always made things worse for everyone around her. Maybe a morning walk would help calm her nerves and refresh her body.

Eli pointed to the mounted television and let milk from his cereal spoon drip onto the farmhouse table. "Hey, Aunt Carli. Look, it's you."

Channel 5 News flashed her photo beside Sadie's.

"Carli Moore, a local woman from Crystal Creek, discovered a body around two p.m. yesterday afternoon, believed to be Sadie Wescott. The corpse was found in a cave located on the Moore family ranch. Remains will be autopsied at the Henderson County coroner's office. Ms. Moore's brother was a person of interest two years ago when Ms. Wescott went missing. After an interview with Detective Steele this morning, it seems Tyler Moore is still their prime suspect."

Carli sat up straighter and increased the volume.

Zain stood right behind Nate with Lieutenant Black to his left. Nate leaned closer to several microphones attached to a podium. He must be the point man on the case. Mechanical cameras clicked trying to grab a good media shot.

"We recovered a body from a local cave on the Moore family ranch property. Our Henderson County coroner will perform an autopsy on the remains. The sheriff's department will not be making any preliminary conclusions until he has completed his exam."

Carli stared at the screen. Flashes of light snapped around Zain, and his face held a somber expression. Hopeless. Defeated. Nate's statement made her feel the same way.

Several voices shouted questions, but a female won her moment over others, directing her question to Zain. "Sergeant Wescott, the victim is allegedly your sister. Is Tyler Moore a person of interest in this case?"

Zain glanced at the lieutenant, who gave him a nod. He stepped to the podium. "He is."

"Will he be taken into custody?"

"We're not able to locate Mr. Moore at this time, but are searching for him. We would like to ask him questions in regard to his property and the body found there."

Marta placed a plate of eggs with a side of bacon in front of Carli. "They're looking for Tyler?"

"Along with everyone else." Carli's appetite

faded into emptiness gnawing at her stomach. She stood and grabbed her cell, bag and the keys to her brother's old truck. She missed her Jeep.

"Well, he said he'd be back at the end of the week. Try calling him again. Let him know about…" Marta's words faded as her worried gaze fell to Eli.

"I will." Carli gave the woman another hug. "We'll all be fine, but first, I need to talk to Zain. Stop this nonsense."

Eli waved his milky spoon in the air again. "Yeah. We don't like nonsense."

Carli popped another piece of bacon in her mouth, headed out the front door and slid into the driver's seat of her brother's old truck. No Bluetooth in this thing. She popped in her earbuds and dialed Tyler's number again. Nothing but his voice mail.

"Call me back, Tyler. This is an emergency."

She started the truck and headed out to the main road with Zain on her mind. She thought they were reconnecting, moving past everything that tore them apart the first time. But he was still the same man, the same officer.

Carli topped the hill providing a view of the town of Crystal Creek looming in front of her.

Most visitors loved the quaint boulevards and the colorful shops, restaurants and art galleries along Main Street. A tourism gold mine for them. Not so much for Carli.

She pulled into a parking spot in front of Heather Barrett's Coffee Bar and tried to work up the courage to enter. Right now, she had to focus on finding Zain.

Carli leaned her head against the seat. Several patrons entered Heather's shop, not giving her truck a second glance. Nerves in her chest tightened as she tried to dig deep for the courage to enter.

Do this for Tyler…and Sadie.

She pressed open the truck door, placed her boots on the ground and walked inside, a dinging bell announcing her arrival. All gazes fell on her with a hush rippling through coffee-scented air.

Skye Anderson, a local post office supervisor, sat to her left, while Dale Hunt, a federal DEA agent in town working a case, nibbled on a croissant at a table with Nate.

Dr. Candyce Frye, dressed in a white lab coat, with a designer bag and shoes to match, greeted her with a smile. Her dark straight hair was fastened with a beautiful jeweled clasp at her neck. Her medical clinic business must be booming. Most people in this town didn't have money to splurge on nice accessories. Of course, the woman was a doctor.

Carli scanned the café for Zain. He stood leaning against the counter, coffee in hand and a stunned look on his face at her presence. Ceiling fans whirled above them and provided white noise to this awkward moment fit for a teenage coming-of-age movie.

Heat crept up Carli's neck and into her cheeks, but she kept her focus on Zain. "Can we talk?"

He nodded and fumbled for his wallet. "Sure. Let me pay."

Heather took his debit card, swiped the reader and cast a glare in her direction. "Zain's a little busy right now."

Carli wasn't there to cause a ruckus with the town barista, but some people needed to learn to keep their noses out of other's business. "I understand, but this is a time-sensitive matter and really has nothing to do with you."

Zain returned his wallet to his back pocket and started toward her, but Heather grabbed his arm. "I think this does involve me since you're in my shop. Sergeant Wescott hasn't finished his coffee. Why don't you run on back to your little ranch or your big city job in Atlanta and leave us all alone?"

Carli stood silent. Not sure what to say. Often, the town's smattering of dislike for her family emerged in silent shunnings. Nothing quite so vocal. But since they'd found Sadie's body, viciousness had increased to a new level.

From the fiery looks aimed in Carli's direction, most of the town must still blame her brother for Sadie's death. Not that Zain's interview this morning helped to squelch any of those rumors.

A trickle of clapping started from the back. She couldn't see who, but others joined. They really did hate her and Tyler. Zain pulled his arm from Heather's grasp, crossed to Carli and escorted her into the street.

He closed the door behind them. "What are you doing? Did you decide you needed a punishment this morning? You should've known they wouldn't treat you well after finding Sadie's body yesterday."

Carli flung her hand toward the store. "And you didn't help sway their opinions of my family with your little show on the news this morning. Tyler's starting to get his life back together with Eli after the questioning from two years ago. Our ranch is performing well and he's providing for his family. If you continue to put this news out, you could ruin our lives."

Zain's jaw tightened and he cut his gaze to hers. "Like someone ruined mine? Wish I still had a chance to take care of my sister. Her sweet life was snuffed out like a flame on a candle. My mother's heart destroyed. Our reputation clouded by an air of disaster. All the locals pity us. I see sympathy in their faces every time I meet someone on the street."

Carli balked at his last statement. "You're not pitied. You're a sergeant with the sheriff's department. They all love you. You'll probably run the whole place one day."

"Not if I don't solve my sister's murder." He let his hands fall to his side. "Listen, Carli. I don't want to fight with you, but I need to talk to Tyler. I know he would never threaten you and we don't have any real evidence against him, but the sheriff's office wants this put to rest quickly. They're willing to take what little they have on Tyler and pin him with the murder. If you want me to prove your brother's innocence, then I need your help."

Could she trust him to help Tyler?

Zain had been so angry two years ago.

She might not remember much from the night her best friend went missing, but she did remember the fight ending her relationship with Zain a few weeks later.

He'd brought Tyler in for questioning, putting him through hours of grueling interrogation. Tempers flared and she ended things. Zain gave her no other choice.

She would always stick by her brother. Tyler had lost his parents and his wife all in one accident. Eli would grow up without his mother. But somehow her brother was the rock that helped her through all the grief. The reading of their parents' will revealed a secret that gave Tyler every right to walk away from her, but he didn't.

He stuck by her...his *adopted* sister.

That's right. She wasn't the biological daughter of Reed and Virginia Moore. A concept that still seemed foreign to her two years later. The only woman she'd ever called Mom revealed the life-altering news through a handwritten letter delivered to her by an estate attorney. The words still burned into her memory. They loved her and would always be her parents, but she was not their biological child. They didn't even mention her real parents' names. No other information was included.

Carli had so many unanswered questions.

Tyler had been kept in the dark also. Yet, he never treated Carli any differently. He'd been true to the words he told her that day: "No matter what, you'll always be my sister and nothing will ever change that, especially not a piece of paper."

She'd fight for her brother no matter what, and if she offered her help, she could keep an eye on the case.

She glanced at the man waiting for her answer. No one in town knew her secret. Not even Zain. She had wanted to tell him back then, but she was afraid he'd look at her differently. No longer a true member of the Moore family, a name that had garnered respect within the Crystal Creek community. She couldn't stand the thought of losing more of the only life she'd ever known. Wasn't the loss of her parents and sister-in-law enough?

She had needed time to figure out this new identity before sharing with others. Then Sadie disappeared and her world turned to chaos.

Carli stepped up closer and lowered her voice to keep people on the street from overhearing. "I'll help you, but if any information I give you starts being used against my brother, I'm out and I'll bring in my lawyer. Understood?"

"Agreed."

"Now tell me why leadership is so determined to pin this on Tyler?"

"He was the last one to see her the night she disappeared and the body's been found on his property, they think that makes him guilty."

Carli motioned toward the old truck and meandered in that direction. "But that's where they're wrong, Sergeant."

"What do you mean?"

"I was the last one to see Sadie on the night she died. I placed my head on the open truck window hoping some cold night air would help my spinning head. Sadie walked back toward the old barn."

"Wait… I thought she went back to the party after she put you in Tyler's truck."

Carli glanced at the mountains surrounding the town and tried to recall the details. "I remember being in her car, bouncing in the back seat. She was driving through the large pasture on our property that's down by the creek. That's where the party was located, just past my daddy's old barn. Danny Mitchell organized the festivities and asked if he could use the space. I gave him permission. Anyway, Sadie drove me through the field and up my long gravel drive. Then she helped Tyler get me in the truck. She left her car parked on the side of the road and walked back toward the old barn."

"Did she go inside?"

The rest of the night faded into a void of emptiness. "I don't know. I can't remember. Why does it matter anyway? She was obviously going back to the party."

"Not necessarily. We've been thinking her killer was someone at the party, but they all have tight alibis. Tyler was the only one unable to substantiate his whereabouts. Plus, a couple of witnesses testified to driving down to the party and said they saw Tyler and Sadie arguing up at the road. He was in her face and angry."

"They were fighting about me. Tyler loved Sadie. He'd never harm her."

"Was there more to that love than you knew?"

A rush of heat surged to her cheeks. "No. They were friends. That's all."

"That's not what some people testified."

"And this town makes up all kinds of stories. According to them, I'm an alcoholic liar who abandoned my family for a job in Atlanta. Do you have any proof?"

Zain shook his head.

"Then I can promise you, Tyler was faithful to his wife and there was never anything romantic going on with Sadie, no matter what the chit-chat was."

They walked a bit farther down the sidewalk in silence, away from a few window shoppers. The last thing she needed was anyone spreading her conversation with Zain through the gossip mill.

Zain stopped in his tracks and Carli glanced at him. She could almost see the thoughts in his head working to make sense of what she told him. At least he was listening.

"Then, if she went into the barn after the argument and you saw her walk there as you were driving away—"

"She might've died in the barn."

"It could be the scene of the crime. I'll go back to the office and look at the case files, see if a thorough search of the old barn was completed.

If we were only looking for a missing person at the time, the team might have overlooked some evidence."

They walked toward her truck. Zain's SUV was only a few spaces from her vehicle. Carli dug into her bag for her brother's spare key, then opened the driver-side door.

Zain kicked her front tire. "You've got a flat?"

Carli closed the door and looked. "Great. I must've run over a nail or something."

Zain ran his fingers along the sidewall of the tire. "I don't think so. Give me your hand."

She hesitated for a moment and then slipped her fingers into his. He pulled her toward the ground as they both squatted side by side in front of the tire.

Carli glanced around, self-conscious of prying eyes, but the other vehicles shielded them from view.

Zain gently ran her fingers over a rough area on the side. A one-inch slit. Made with the blade of a knife, not a nail and not the first time her tire had been slashed. For some reason, being here with Zain, her hand in his, diminished the annoyance factor.

"Someone slashed it?"

His blue eyes drifted up her arm and met her gaze, tingling nerves into her spine. She licked her lips with a dry tongue.

"Looks that way." He hesitated and kept her fingers in his. "I can change it, if you want."

Time seemed to slow. She didn't want to move, to break the moment, but she had to. They'd tried to make things work before and everything ended in disaster. Her heart broken in a million pieces.

She pulled her hand from his and moved to the truck, pulling out her brother's toolbox.

"You got a tire iron?" he asked.

"A tire iron?" Carli flipped open the latch and pulled out a cordless drill. "Why use a manual tool when you can use an impact drill?"

Zain shook his head with a smile. "You never cease to surprise me, Carli Moore. Most women don't even know what an impact drill is."

"Well, I'm not most women."

She squatted back down beside him and handed him the drill, placing the case to the side. His gaze caught hers again, this time tinged with the hint of a smile. "That's the truth."

Zain leaned toward her. Surely, he wasn't going to kiss her.

He reached past her and grabbed a socket for the drill.

Heat rose to her cheeks at the premature thought. "Sorry. I forgot about the socket."

"No worries."

Footsteps rounded the car next to them. "Hey. What are you two doing down there?"

Detective Nate Steele stood behind them with his keys in hand. He was the same age as Zain, lighter hair, but handsome in a good ole country boy kind of way. The two men graduated from the local community college with a degree in basic law enforcement. They'd been partners together at the sheriff's office for years, until Zain was promoted to sergeant and Nate joined his forensics team as a detective.

Carli stood. "Nothing. Just changing my tire." She fingered the long silver chain with a butterfly locket that dangled from her neck.

"Cool necklace."

"Thanks. It was a gift from Sadie. She gave it to me the night she died."

Zain paused the drill and glanced up at the trinket, but said nothing.

Nate leaned against the fender of the truck. "Nice you have something to remember her by. Y'all were pretty close, weren't you?"

"She was my best friend. We grew up together. Neighbors, but more like sisters."

"I guess you miss her, huh?"

The familiar grief burned at the corners of her eyes. "Every day."

Zain paused again. "Hey, Nate. You want to get me the spare out of the back?"

"Sure."

Zain stood while his friend went to the back

of the truck, and he glanced at Carli's necklace, lifted the locket in his fingers. "This was my sister's?"

A sad tone hung in his question. "Yeah." Carli swallowed, fighting the urge to comfort him with a hug. "Do you remember her wearing it?"

"Vaguely. Not really something an older brother cares about, until his sister's not around anymore."

An exhausted pain filled his expression. When had he last smiled or laughed? Did he carry the burden of Sadie's death with him everywhere he went?

She did.

Nate rolled the tire up behind him. "Here ya go."

Zain let the locket drop against her shirt and helped position the spare into place. Their moment, over.

Zain ducked his head and peered under the car. "That's not good."

Carli squatted beside him for a better view. A black box with blinking red lights was attached to the frame.

"What's that?"

Zain grabbed the device and pulled it free. "GPS tracker. Now we know how they found you on the parkway last night. Got a plastic bag?"

"Probably. Tyler keeps all kinds of junk in the back seat." Carli climbed inside and shuffled through the mess. An old plastic grocery bag poked out from the side door compartment. She handed it to Zain.

He slipped the device inside. "I'll take it to the station. Have it checked for fingerprints."

Carli stared at the bag. This was more than the town not liking her or her brother. More than being bullied by mean-spirited people. Whoever killed Sadie wouldn't stop until he finished the job and Carli was dead.

Carli retrieved her phone from her pocket and pulled up the threatening text, handing the cell to Zain. "I think you might want to read this."

FOUR

Zain pulled his truck to a stop and cut the headlights. Twilight framed the Moore family's new barn in a dusky haze. The structure was massive. Two stories of steel and wood situated fifty feet from the older barn. Must've been forty feet wide by eighty in length.

Zain stepped from his truck and entered through the open door. The main aisle was large with an office, bathroom, and ten stalls for horses shooting off to the sides. Business must be booming.

"Carli?"

She poked her head out of one of the back rooms, her auburn braid resting on her shoulder. "Back here."

Zain walked toward the stall and Carli glanced up from checking Cocoa's hooves. "I didn't expect you to come by after everything that happened this morning at the coffee shop."

"I wanted to make sure you were okay."

"To be honest, I'm still a bit shaken up about the GPS tracker. Coming out here with Cocoa helps me clear my head, ya know?"

Zain leaned against the locked door and petted Cocoa's nose through the metal bars. He did know. Something about the Moore family ranch had always provided a sense of peace for him too.

Cocoa snorted and Carli laughed, as she picked up a brush and stroked the animal's side. "No worries, Cocoa. You know Sergeant Wescott." She motioned toward a pail hanging next to him. "There's a couple of carrots if you want to feed him while I brush."

Zain pulled out a treat and let Cocoa nibble the end. Memories of his past days riding horses with Carli and cleaning out stalls flashed through his mind.

He wished they could go back to that simpler time, like when he was twelve years old and she rode over on the back of a pony to introduce herself. His parents had talked about the new family for weeks before they got there. He prayed for another boy close to his age since he didn't have a brother, but when he saw Carli, he was smitten.

Her natural beauty had only increased with time. Experience and tragedy had developed a strong heart, with a body of curves and green eyes he could stare at forever. Her long fingers held the brush moving in rhythmic strokes across Cocoa's shiny coat.

She had an easy way with horses. This ranch was where Carli fit. The big city of Atlanta didn't match the girl he knew.

"Did you find anything on the GPS or the texts?" Carli asked, bringing his thoughts back to the moment.

"Not really. There were no prints and the tracker itself was about as generic as they come. Could have bought it from hundreds of different places. The texts were from a burner, but I asked the cyber team to take a look. That takes a while."

"Then we're not any closer to finding out who's targeting me. Great."

"We'll find this person. I promise. I'm not going to let anybody hurt you."

She kept brushing and didn't look at him. He hoped his words sounded more confident than he felt. Truth was he didn't know how Sadie's death and the threats on Carli's life fit together, but he wasn't about to stop trying to figure it out. If only she could remember more from the party.

The night might've been a blur for Carli, but he remembered every detail. They were supposed to attend together, but instead they got in a huge fight when she told him about her job in Atlanta. Said she had to prove herself and honor her parents' memory. What did she have to prove?

"I know you said you don't remember much about the night of the party, but do you remember why you were adamant about going to Atlanta?"

Her hand slowed her strokes over Cocoa's fur. She avoided his gaze, like she was keeping something from him. "I guess I never told you."

"Never told me what?"

She shrugged. "The day of the Summer's End party, Tyler and I met with my parents' estate lawyers. We should've gone months before, but we were both in such shock at the loss in our family, we never got around to it until then. They split everything fifty-fifty between Tyler and me. Then the lawyers handed me a handwritten letter from my mother. The letter stated I was adopted."

Had he heard wrong? Carli adopted? "What?"

She stretched out an arm in his direction. "Yep. Moore family blood does not course through these veins."

Cocoa huffed and Carli went back to brushing. "The news almost destroyed me. The parents I loved had been lying to me my whole life and now they were gone. I had no way to reconcile their secret with all the questions that arose from the news. I needed to get away, to escape and figure out who I really was. Atlanta seemed like as good of an option as any, and they were offering me a salary I couldn't refuse."

Zain fumbled for another carrot to feed Cocoa. "Did the letter tell you who your biological parents were?"

"There was nothing about them, and I'm not sure I want to know. I have a great life and the people who raised me are still my parents. Always will be. My birth parents chose to give me up, so I'm not sure I want to have people like that in my life."

"That's a pretty strong decision."

"It's been two years and I've had a lot of time to think about it, but that night at the party, I was not in good shape. Sadie didn't want to go, but after the fight with you, I needed a distraction. I begged her to go with me."

Carli raised her glassy eyes to his. "If I'd been less selfish and stayed home to watch movies like she wanted, Sadie would still be here with us today."

Zain flattened his hand to let Cocoa finish off the end of the carrot. He understood the guilt she felt. He held his own mistakes from that night he had to overcome. "There's always what-if scenarios that bring on the shame. You can't let yourself go there."

"That's my problem. Too often I live in that

space, and coming back to Crystal Creek only magnifies the shame of my decisions."

"Did Tyler know you were adopted?"

She glanced over at him. "Found out the same day I did when we were at the lawyer's office. He was great. Told me as far as he's concerned, I would always be his little sister. He never treated me any different."

Score a few points for the brother.

"Let's walk through the night of the party again. You and Sadie arrived and you had a few too many drinks…right?"

Carli shook her head and moved to the other side of the horse to brush. "Only one drink. Someone handed me the cup. I thought it was punch, but it must've been spiked because it tasted funny. I drank about half of it and threw out the rest."

"Half of a spiked drink would not make anyone forget the entire night."

"Then how do you explain me not being able to remember anything?"

The report details said Tyler took his sister home, carried her to bed because Carli was unable to walk. Then her brother went back to the party to look for Sadie. When he didn't find Sadie, he figured she caught another ride. He returned home and Carli was still unconscious, but stable. Something didn't add up.

"Carli, I think your drink was drugged."

"More than just some joker pouring the contents of a flask into the punch bowl?"

"Yeah. Didn't your parents and sister-in-law attend a charity function the night they died?"

"The Children's Cancer Ball. They attended every year. But what does that have to do with my drink being drugged?"

"A witness from that event stated your father didn't feel well and they headed home early. If he was drugged too, then that could be why he ran off the road on the parkway."

She moved to the stall door and faced him. "You think someone planned the same for me?"

"I think it's a good possibility. Especially since you're sure you only had one drink."

"But my parents died three months before Sadie disappeared. Why would someone want them dead?"

"I dug into their case report today. Most of it was standard for an accident, but then I found a note that your parents had set up a meeting with the sheriff. They wanted to discuss the increase in prescription drug distribution in the town, but died two days before they were to meet with him."

Carli rubbed her fingers across the bristles of the brush and plucked a few hairs from the side, then swiped a tear from her cheek with the back of her hand. "Do you think Sadie's death might be tied to my parents'? She was a nurse manager at Dr. Frye's office. She could've discovered something also being in the health-care environment."

"I don't know yet. But definitely an avenue I'll be looking into. Prescription drug abuse has spiked over the last few years. We've arrested several people in the town for distribution."

"That's comforting," she said sarcastically and tossed the horse brush into its bag. "All Sadie wanted to do that night was take care of me."

One of the things Zain loved about his sister—her willingness to take care of others, especially their mother when she was sick. "I wish I could've saved her."

"You and me both."

"I could've done more, ya know. If Nate and I had followed through with my assignment then she might still be here. Sometimes the guilt is unbearable."

"What do you have to feel guilty for? Being the best brother ever?"

Her words couldn't be further from the truth. He exhaled an audible sigh. "After our fight the night of the party, I decided to pull an extra third shift. My sergeant told me and Nate to go break up the party. Your brother called in the tip."

A smile tweaked the corner of Carli's lips. "I didn't know that."

"He didn't like you being there. Figured if he let the cops break it up, he wouldn't be the bad guy in your eyes. Anyway, we'd just ordered our food at Mama's Diner on Main Street and were starving. A couple of other deputies, Harris and King, were on their way out. We passed the task off to them. I always wondered if I'd gone, would Sadie still be with us? I could've brought her home."

Carli flicked her gaze in his direction, grabbed a different brush and continued to run her hands over Cocoa's side. "Like you said, there will always be what-if scenarios."

"How did you handle losing your parents and your best friend all within a matter of months?"

"I can't explain it, except God provided me the comfort I needed to get through. He didn't keep bad things from happening, but He sustained me while everything was chaos. If I have any strength, it's from Him."

Zain didn't know what to say. His relationship with God was almost nonexistent since his sister's disappearance. His mother tried to get him to go to church with her, but for some reason, he couldn't.

"I'm not sure I'll feel any peace until Sadie's killer is behind bars."

Carli gave Cocoa a kiss on the nose and stepped outside of the stall. She didn't respond to his statement. Maybe she was tired of talking about the case. Instead, she handed him a halter and pointed to a peg on the wall. "Can you hang that for me?"

"Sure."

Zain did as instructed, then turned back to face her. She brushed the dust from her jeans and straightened with a knee-weakening smile. "You hungry?"

"I thought you'd never ask. Whatever Marta was fixing when I stopped by earlier smelled amazing."

"I think tonight's menu is jambalaya."

"Great. We can discuss the 24-7 detail I'll be assigning to you over a good, fiery Cajun meal."

Carli let out an exasperated sigh and pulled her vibrating phone from her pocket. Her eyes widened when she glanced at the screen. Zain leaned closer for a better view.

A photo of Eli playing in the kitchen displayed with a message.

Give up the necklace or Eli's next.

Carli stepped on the gas, vibrations from the gravel road underneath her feet. Marta and Eli were in the house alone. Her nephew chose the

Batman shirt he wore today, now on full display in the image. Someone had taken the photo within the last hour.

She never dreamed anyone would come after Eli. If he was in danger, then they needed Zain's help to keep Eli safe.

Zain typed on his phone and then shoved it into his pocket. "Nate's on his way. He's five minutes out. Should get there right after us."

Carli kept one hand on the wheel while she dug into the console of the truck and retrieved the pistol kept there. She pointed toward the glove compartment.

"There's extra ammo in there."

Zain didn't hesitate to grab the additional rounds for her weapon, handing them to her, then pulling his own firearm from his holster.

What would someone want with the necklace Sadie gave her? The piece was custom-made with a braided silver chain and a turquoise butterfly locket attached. Might have some value, but nothing to threaten a child over.

Headlight beams bounced over the field when they hit deep ruts from a recent rain. Carli didn't slow down, instead she plowed across the divots, bouncing her and Zain inside the cab.

Eli was in trouble. Whoever taunted her had crossed a line. Protective instincts raged within, igniting a fury she'd never felt before.

Gravel slung to the side as she rounded the bend. Zain white-knuckled the roll cage above his head, but kept quiet about her driving. His gaze scoured the landscape. Probably searching for any intruders on the premises.

The sprawling two-story craftsman home came into view. The glow of kitchen lights spilled across the manicured lawn. Marta and Eli danced around inside the kitchen, oblivious to the terror coursing through every nerve in Carli's body. At least they were safe and alive. For now.

Each held the end of a dishcloth, laughing. Darkened windows in the rest of the house obscured any view of an intruder.

Carli slowed her course. "Do you see anyone?"

Zain leaned forward but didn't respond. His gaze lifted to the second story, and he pointed. "Upstairs."

A dim night-light plugged into the bedroom wall cast a silhouette against the curtain covering the window. A shadowy figure moved inside Carli's bedroom. She flashed her headlights in an effort to scare them away. They moved out of sight.

"We've got to get Eli and Marta out of there."

She slammed the truck to a halt, bailed from the seat and sprinted across the gravel drive. Zain stayed on her heels. Pebbles crunched underneath their steps as they pounded closer to the back entrance. Carli's grip tightened on her weapon.

Zain motioned toward the door handle. "You remember how to clear a room?"

Something they used to do for fun on date nights. "Just like you taught me."

He nodded. "If anyone takes your gun—"

"I go for the eyes and throat."

Zain gripped the doorknob. "You go first. Get to Marta and Eli, take them outside, and I'll meet you in the yard after I clear the upstairs."

"Take the back staircase. It's faster."

Zain pushed the door open and Carli breeched the entrance, gun raised ready for any attacker. Her father taught her to shoot. Only clay discs and old cans back in the day, but she won multiple target competitions all through her teen years. Not many in town could beat her aim.

Except Zain.

But she had never killed another human before. Zain had. She didn't know how many. After the first one, he never mentioned the dark parts of his job again. She shuddered at the thought of taking someone's life, but if anyone threatened her nephew, she wouldn't hesitate to pull the trigger.

The hall seemed longer than normal and every room a potential threat. She cleared each space and moved toward the open great room with the kitchen off to the side. Marta and Eli were still there, singing at the tops of their lungs. Some old song played on the radio, a fifties classic.

She moved into the kitchen and tucked her gun into the back of her jeans. "Hi, guys." They both turned around and started giggling.

Glad someone could laugh despite the lurking danger. "How about we take the showstopper into the yard."

Eli began jumping up and down. "Can I catch lightning bugs too?"

"Of course."

Marta shot her a confused look. Usually after dinner cleanup, Eli had his bath and she read him stories, but tonight was different. Marta didn't argue.

Carli stepped onto the outdoor rock patio and swept Eli into her arms. "Let's run fast."

"Come on, Marta, run with us," Eli said.

Carli rounded the corner of the house and stopped short. The glow from the living room lamps highlighted Nate's face at the other end of the porch, gun raised.

Carli lifted a free hand. "Don't shoot. It's me."

The detective relaxed and put his gun into his holster. Zain stepped around her into view. "Anything?"

Nate shook his head. "I checked the back shed and fence line. I didn't see anyone."

Marta leaned against the railing. "What are you talking about?"

Zain rubbed the back of his neck. "He escaped from the house too. Must've had a vehicle."

Marta put her hands on her hips and stomped a foot. "Would someone please tell me what's going on?"

"Sorry. I didn't want to scare you earlier, but there was an intruder in our house, my bedroom, specifically."

Eli looked at Carli's necklace and pushed the locket with his finger. "What's an intruder?"

The last thing she wanted was for Eli to be afraid in his own home. Tyler wasn't here to comfort him. How much could a five-year-old handle? She'd never let anything happen to him while she was here and tried to think of the appropriate words to explain their situation.

"Someone who came for a visit unannounced, baby. That's all. Why don't you go catch those lightning bugs you talked about? Just stay close. Okay?"

"Okay."

"Nate, will you go with him?" Carli asked, still shaken by the whole ordeal.

"Sure."

The boy took off with his arms out to the side like an airplane. Nate followed. She waited until

Eli was out of earshot then faced Zain. "What did he take from my bedroom?"

"Nothing that I can tell, but the room's been ransacked. If they're after your necklace, then I guess they didn't find it, but you'll have to look around and see if anything else is missing."

She lifted the chain from her shirt. "Why would they want my necklace? It's a silver chain with a butterfly locket."

Zain leaned in for a closer look. "Beats me, but they were pretty specific in the text. Have you received any more threats?"

"No."

Marta stepped up closer. "What threats?"

Both ignored her question. "I guess your tires getting slashed this morning was a threat in itself."

"Your tires were slashed?" Marta paled with each bit of information.

Carli patted the older woman's arm in an effort to reassure her, but kept her focus on Zain. "I'm fine. Zain was with me."

Marta straightened. "Then Zain must stay here around the clock. I will not have my Carli and Eli in danger."

Before Carli could protest, Marta had her hand wrapped around Zain's arm. "There's a bed in our sunroom porch on the front of the house.

You can sleep there and use the bathroom off the living area."

If Carli didn't speak up then her ex-boyfriend would be her new roommate. Not something she wanted to happen. "Forgive me, Marta, but Zain doesn't want to stay with us. He has his mother to take care of."

Zain turned on the porch toward her. "My mom's doing fine and I can check on her before and after work. It would only be until Tyler returns which should be a couple of weeks, right?"

"No offense, but if this town gets wind of you protecting me, you'll be demoted for sure. We can't have that. Might need you to run for sheriff one day."

"Your safety is what matters, not my career."

He leaned against her railing in his tight jeans, his toned biceps folded across his gray T-shirt. Every muscle defined. His eyes softened with genuine concern for their safety, the color of blue persuading her to let him stay.

Eli ran onto the porch with his hands cupped. "Look, Aunt Carli. I caught one. I caught a lightning bug."

"Open your fingers and let me see."

The winged creature crawled onto the tip of Eli's finger, spread its wings and flew back into the night sky to join the others across the yard.

A symphony of lights spread out before her.

A beautiful sight.

Until the dark shadow against the tree line moved.

"He's still here." She lifted Eli into her arms and retreated into the house. Zain and Nate sped off in the SUV toward the dark horizon.

Marta followed her inside and wrapped an arm around Carli's shoulders as she watched the glowing taillights move down the driveway.

"Having Zain here might be awkward, but we need him to stay. I don't know what I would do if anything happened to you or Eli."

Carli put her arm around the woman. "I know."

FIVE

Zain took the pillow Carli handed him and tried to slide on the outside casing. The shadowy figure against the tree line had disappeared without a trace.

Nate and a couple of other deputies had completed another perimeter check of the area. Some SUV tracks were found leading out to the back road on the property, but no cars were in sight once they hit the main road.

Carli unfolded a clean fitted sheet. "Do you think he'll come back tonight?"

"I don't know. Probably not, but I think it's best if we keep a watch for a few days."

She tucked the deep pockets around the corners of the mattress and smoothed her hands over the sheets to get out the wrinkles. "I hope you don't mind sleeping in the sunroom. Tyler only has one guest room and I'm sleeping there, so this is all we've got."

He hadn't slept on an enclosed porch in a long

time. The pillow and blanket he held to his chest smelled like her, fresh with a hint of vanilla. "I can sleep about anywhere. Dad used to take me and Sadie camping. He'd give us a pillow and a sleeping bag, then we'd crash on the ground for a couple of days. He said it would make us tough."

"Did it?"

"Nope. Only made me cranky."

Carli laughed. He loved the sound and joined her. She had a way of bringing joy into every moment. Not something he'd had much of since she left.

Carli pointed to one of the bed corners closest to him. "What are you waiting for? An invitation? Secure the sheet please."

Her tone was teasing but serious. "Yes, ma'am."

She straightened with her hands on her hips. "You did *not* just call me ma'am, did you?"

He forced a serious look onto his face and shrugged his shoulders. "Sorry. My momma always taught me to say ma'am."

Carli stepped around the bed and stood within inches of him. They hadn't spent this much time together since she left for Atlanta two years ago. She snagged the blue quilt from his hands, letting her fingers brush his. He wished she'd let them linger.

"How is your mother, by the way?"

He grabbed the other pillow and finagled it into the case. "She's doing okay. Still weak from all the chemo and radiation. I'm not sure she'll ever get back to her normal energy level, but Dr. Frye has her taking vitamin D supplements and B12 shots. She seems a bit perkier lately. At least she's getting out and doing things now. I'm thankful she's in remission."

"I'm so glad to hear that. At least Sadie was able to help her while she was here."

A familiar heaviness swirled through him at the mention of his sister's name. "She did so much for Mom. Paid for most of her treatments."

"The girl did have an amazing business mind."

"She *was* a mathematical whiz. Never once asked me for money, although I often gave her what I could. The salary of a deputy didn't go far. She rarely left Mom's side while she was doing chemo."

Carli folded down the top of the quilt. "Well, she was a nurse and took care of patients every day at Dr. Frye's office. It was only natural for her to want to do the same for your mom."

"She was always like that, even when we were kids. One time our cat got ahold of some baby rabbits. Their eyes weren't even open yet, and Sadie brought them home, fed them goat's milk from an eyedropper and kept them underneath a heat lamp until they were old enough to be released into our yard." His fingers dug into the pillow he held. "Every time I see a rabbit these days, I think of her. What I wouldn't give to have her back."

Carli crossed over to him, placed the pillow on the bed and wrapped her arms around him like she had in the cave. Comfort washed through him. She smelled of sweet vanilla like the quilt.

"I miss her too." Her breath was hot against his chest.

Zain pulled back. Light spilled through the kitchen window and highlighted the pink flush of Carli's cheeks. Her green eyes sparkled and creased at the corners from a smile, sweet enough to make any man weak. Cicadas chirped their night song as if encouraging him to follow his instincts. He leaned forward, but Carli pressed a hand against his chest, stepping back. Her gaze fell to the floor.

"Zain, we can't. We've been here before and it didn't work. Once Tyler returns, I'll head back to Atlanta. My life is there now."

She was right. What was he thinking? There were too many obstacles for them to overcome.

He held up his hands. "I apologize. I was out of line."

She relaxed her body back against the bedpost. "It's not that, I just—"

"Aunt Carli. Where are you? I'm scared."

Small feet pattered across the great room floor. Carli moved farther from Zain and met Eli at the screen door. Hinges squeaked open and Carli lifted the boy into her arms. His red curls, still wet from his bath, plus cute Batman pajamas tugged at Zain's heart. Any frustration from the moment was forgotten.

Carli gave Eli a kiss on the cheek. "Can you tell Sergeant Wescott good night?"

Her nephew placed a hand to his forehead in a salute and lowered his voice as deep as it would go. "Good night, Sergeant Wescott."

"Night, bud."

Carli gave a small wave. "If you need anything else, text me. I'll leave my phone on."

He picked up the pillow she'd placed on the bed. "About earlier."

"Don't worry about it. We're good."

She smiled and slipped inside the home.

Zain fell back on the bed and exhaled. This was not the time to get swept up with emotions or they'd both likely end up dead. He had to focus and figure out the identity of the intruder. That way, Carli could return home to Atlanta and he could get on with his life.

He pulled his phone from his backpack. Time was only 9:00 p.m. Dr. Sam Kendrick, the medical examiner, worked the evening shift and should be at his office. Maybe Zain could get an update since sleep was the furthest thing from his mind.

The phone rang three times before the man picked up. "No, I haven't completed my report on the body found in the cave yet and no matter how many times you call, I will not rush."

"But you've got *something* you can tell me, right?"

The pause on the other end of the line confirmed Zain's suspicions. "It's Sadie, isn't it?"

Kendrick sighed into the phone. "You know I don't like giving out preliminary results, but I'll make an exception this one time, since the case involves your sister."

"Noted."

"The dental work matched the records you provided from Sadie."

Sam's words pierced through Zain's tough exterior. No matter how many times he'd imagined this scenario, even planned on hearing these very words, nothing alleviated the pain tied to the facts presented. Walls he'd built for his own emotional protection were destroyed with Kendrick's one statement.

His sister was officially dead.

A thick sob formed in his throat. He pushed it down and tried to treat this like any other case. He needed more information to find her killer. "Anything else you can tell me?"

"Cause of death was blunt force trauma. And we found a gum wrapper in her sweater pocket."

Zain sat up on the side of the bed at the news. "What kind?"

"You want to know the brand?"

"Yeah."

Papers shuffled in the background with a few intermittent mouse clicks. "Looks like it was a Hot Red wrapper."

"That brand is still around?"

"I'd have to do a bit of research but I believe it's only sold in novelty shops in the South and those country store restaurants trying to keep the good ole days alive. A little harder to find, but if your sister liked the gum, she would know where to get a pack."

Zain jotted down the notes on an old paper pad left on a side table. "That's cinnamon flavored, right?"

"Yeah, why do you ask?"

"My sister was allergic to cinnamon and hated anything remotely close to the real spice. I don't think the wrapper belonged to her."

"You're probably right."

"Thanks for the info."

"Should have my official report completed and submitted tomorrow."

"See, I wasn't rushing you."

"Things have been a little light lately. And

truth be told, I met your sister once when she was at a conference with Dr. Frye. A lovely lady."

"Thanks, Sam. Have a good night."

Zain ended the call and kept brainstorming with the information Dr. Kendrick gave him.

He needed to find Tyler, to see if anything he remembered might help him find who was threatening Carli.

Zain scrolled through his contacts until he found Dale Hunt's number. They weren't the best of friends, but the man had connections.

"Hey, man, can you do me a favor and keep it quiet? Just between us," Zain asked.

"Absolutely. Whatcha need?"

"I need you to find someone for me. He's wanted for questioning in one of our cases. Thought with your resources, you could track him down."

"What's the name?"

Zain hesitated and looked back toward the door of Carli's house. "Tyler Moore."

Carli fumbled for her phone on the nightstand, her brain annoyed at the buzzing sound and disturbance of sleep. The clock read 2:00 a.m. Was Zain calling her?

She squinted and tried to focus her blurred vision on the name. Tyler.

Her body sprang to life and she hit the accept

key. "I've been trying to call you for days now. Where are you?"

"Hi to you too, sis."

Carli glanced over her shoulder at the sleeping toddler crashed beside her. Eli didn't even budge when she sat up in bed and turned on the lamp. Poor thing. He was exhausted from having a nightmare. At least it seemed the bad dreams were gone for now.

"Tyler Moore. This is no joke. I've been worried sick about you. Why haven't you returned any of my calls?"

Carli flung her side of the sheets back and paced to her bedroom windows overlooking the moonlit creek winding along the back edge of the property. She lowered her voice to keep from waking Eli.

"Calm down. My phone broke and I had to get to a store to get a new one."

"Dallas has tons of phone stores. You couldn't just waltz in and buy one of those at any time of the day or night?" Her frustration filled the sarcastic question, but she was annoyed.

"I'm not in Dallas."

Carli stopped her pacing and stared at the spotlighted ripples curving underneath their covered bridge. "What do you mean you aren't in Dallas?"

"The business deal there fell through, but something opened up in California. I've been traveling for the past couple of days to a ranch around Sonoma Valley. You should see the horses they have here, Carli. Top quality, beautiful Arabians, like ours. Listen, the ranch has been doing really well and I think—"

"Tyler—" The last thing she wanted to hear about right now was Arabian horses.

"What?"

She hesitated for a second. His life was good right now and Carli was about to rob him of his joy. But he had to know.

"We found Sadie's body. She's dead."

Several seconds of silence paused between them. Carli glanced at her screen to see if they were still connected. "You there?"

"Yeah. Just processing. Where'd they find her?"

"In the cave on our property—"

"But they searched the cave when she first disappeared. She wasn't in there then and now the body suddenly appears?"

"Zain thinks whoever killed her moved her there from the original crime scene."

"The good sergeant always has a theory," Tyler said, sarcasm dripping in his tone.

"You need to come home, Tyler. The sheriff's department is looking for you and Zain has some questions, plus, we had an intruder threaten Eli and break into the house."

"What? Is Eli okay?"

"Yes, he's fine. Zain's here, stationed on the front porch."

"Zain Wescott, the man who accused me of killing his sister, is in my house?"

"Look, I don't have time for territorial games. We've been getting threats and after someone broke in tonight, I'm not taking any chances. Eli is scared and frankly, I am too. When are you coming home?"

A scraping noise reverberated through the phone. "Tyler?"

"I'm throwing my things into my suitcase as we speak, but Carli?"

"Yeah."

"It's going to take me a few days to drive home from California. Can you hold down the fort until then?"

"Of course. I've got through next week off. If I need to take more I can. I've still got a couple weeks saved up. Sheila's been on me to schedule all my vacation time anyway."

"Thanks. I know Marta will be happy to have you there longer."

Carli cast an over-the-shoulder glance back at Eli sleeping in her bed. "She's been an amazing help with him during the day while I take care of ranch business. Tonight, he ended up sleeping in my bed because of a nightmare about the intruder."

"Give him a kiss for me. Tell him I'll be home soon."

"Will do."

"One more thing. There's something I need to discuss with you when I get home."

A shadow moved beside the pylon of the covered bridge. Did the wind blow a bush or was it an animal? Carli clicked off the lamp and tried to blink away the temporary light spots from her vision. Nothing there. Must've been an animal. She refocused on Tyler's previous statement.

"What do you need to talk to me about?"

"I don't want to get into it over the phone and if I'm going to get there in a week, I need to get moving. I'll pack tonight, grab a few hours' sleep and head out first thing in the morning."

"Be safe and I love ya, bro."

"Back at ya, sis."

Carli hit the end key and took another look at the bridge.

There was movement. A shadowed figure rose to full height then bent over again. Almost as if he were walking toward the house.

Carli fumbled her fingers over the screen to Zain's number.

Someone's coming up the path.

From the bridge. About five hundred yards away.

Three dots rippled across her screen.

Get Eli and stay put. I'll check it out.

Eli's asleep. Marta can stay with him.
I'm coming with you.

Carli grabbed her Glock from the gun safe and a couple of extra magazines, then headed down the hall to Marta's room. The woman opened the door on the third knock, her dark hair loose about her shoulders.

"Carli, it's two thirty in the morning. What are you doing?"

"I need you to go to my room and stay with Eli."

Marta's gaze fell to the firearm in Carli's hand. Her eyes grew big and she pulled her shaky fingers to her lips. "Why? What's going on?"

"Probably nothing. But Zain and I need to check something out. Please go to my room, lock the door and don't open it for anyone other than me. Okay? Eli's asleep there."

The woman swished past Carli and did as instructed. The bedroom door clicked and Carli descended the stairs.

Zain stood on the edge of the porch, one gun in

hand, the other in his shoulder holster. "I texted you back. Told you to stay locked in the house."

"I didn't see your message. Doesn't matter anyway, I'm coming with you. If someone's out there, I want to stop them before they can get close to Eli. And you might need backup."

After their earlier brush with the intruder, Carli wasn't taking any chances of the guy getting away.

Zain pressed his lips together and racked the slide on his nine-millimeter. "Fine. Let's go."

Carli followed Zain down the stairs and out to the backyard. A forest of trees lined the edge of Crystal Creek and provided cover for them along the same path where she'd last seen the intruder.

Water rushed nearby, nature's white noise for their trek, covering any small sounds they might make on their way. Moonlight sprinkled through the trees and mottled the old farm road, providing light for the path.

Zain held up his hand and slowed her approach. A dark-dressed figure stood oblivious to the nearness of their location, digging into pebbled soil underneath the bridge. The clank and slip of dirt cut into the crickets' nocturnal song.

What was he doing?

Tree limbs blocked Carli's vision. She stepped forward and rolled a branch beneath her shoe. A crack from the dead wood split the night air.

Carli froze.

The masked man pivoted at the sound and faced them, his shovel dropping to the ground with a clang. An arm rose with a glint of metal reflecting in the moonlight.

Carli, petrified, stood rooted to her spot while Zain dropped to his knees. "Get down!"

She raised her gun but was too late.

Gunfire flashed.

Heat seared her thigh.

Carli grabbed her leg and collapsed beneath the cover of a bush. Blood seeped into her jeans. Hot and wet, tingeing the ivory skin on her hands to red. She pulled off her outer shirt and pressed it to the wound.

"Carli!"

Zain discharged a couple of rounds and rushed to her side, large tree trunks providing a shield from the flying bullets chasing him. He knelt down and ripped a larger hole in her jeans.

"Looks like a flesh wound." He glanced over his shoulder. "We need to get you back to the house."

An engine roared to life and headlights glared across the field. A dark-colored van with tinted windows sped to the gravel road, leaving dust for them to breathe.

Carli coughed and tried to push up. "He's getting away. Go after him."

Zain stared at her. "Are you crazy? There's no

way I'm leaving you when you're injured. He's not headed toward the house because he took the back road out. Probably headed to the main highway."

Zain took the bloody shirt from her hand and ripped it into two pieces. One piece he wadded into a ball, and the other strip he tied tight around her leg, securing the homemade bandage in place. "Maybe that will slow down the bleeding until I can get you to the hospital. Do you think you can walk?"

"I can try."

Carli leaned against Zain's side as he lifted her to her feet. She placed her hand on his shoulder for stability, his strength evident. Another quality she found difficult to resist. He started out slow with her, giving time for her to hop on her good leg. At this rate, morning would beat them home.

Carli started to giggle.

He glanced in her direction. "You've been shot and you're bleeding, profusely I might add, so what could you possibly be laughing about?"

"Nerves or maybe us limping along. I'm not sure."

"Aren't you in pain?"

"Burns like my leg's on fire. I'm trying not to think about it."

"So, you laugh?"

"Reminds me of the time we were in the

three-legged race together during vacation Bible school. Do you remember?"

"Seems like we came in first place. Got a trophy."

"And you kissed my cheek after we won."

"I did. I was happy we beat Bobby Baxter. Remember him? He won all the sports trophies back in the day."

"Except ours."

He adjusted her arm to support her weight a bit more. "You were a good partner."

Carli feigned a look of shock. "Oh please, you practically dragged me to the finish line. I fell halfway through and you kept going, pulling me along, kind of like now."

Zain adjusted his hand around her waist and chuckled. "I guess so."

Fatigue crept into her body and she rested her head on his shoulder. Good Zain. Always there for her. Leaving him was the biggest regret of her life.

She made another hop. Pain shot up her leg. Her energy faded. She slowed her movements.

"Carli, are you okay?"

"I'm tired. How much farther?"

"Almost there."

Carli tried to keep moving. Her vision swirled. She let her body collapse against his. Zain must've sensed her inability to function. His body shifted beside hers and he lifted her into his arms.

SIX

Zain clung to Carli and tried to hurry up the hill. Blood continued to seep into her jeans and her usual chatty nature faded.

He needed to get her leg bandaged before the wound became infected. The hospital was thirty minutes away. She'd lose too much blood if he tried to get her there without treating her first.

Why had he let her come? He knew better.

He was supposed to protect her, not put her in more danger.

The back door creaked as he slipped through the kitchen and into the great room. Zain placed Carli on the couch, retrieved a first aid kit and a cup, filled a plastic container with warm, soapy water then grabbed a pair of scissors. He placed several towels under her leg and cut her jeans to expose more of the injury.

"Definitely a flesh wound. I can clean it, but you should go to the hospital."

Carli shook her head. "No. Too far."

He needed to bandage her up now and get some fluids into her. How was he going to start an IV? He'd never done that before and he doubted she had one lying around.

Zain grabbed his phone. "Looks like it might need stitches. Even though there's no bullet, the wound's pretty deep."

Carli's eyes were closed again. He rubbed her cheek with the back of his fingers. Her skin soft to the touch. He'd never forgive himself if anything happened to her on his watch. "Honey, I need you to stay with me. Don't go to sleep yet, okay?"

She barely moved. Her eyes still closed.

"Carli, I need you to wake up."

Nothing.

Zain shifted her body and rested her foot on the ottoman, then he positioned the pan of water on the floor underneath her injured thigh. With a cup full of sudsy water, he poured the liquid over the wound, letting the excess drain back into the plastic tub.

Carli's eyelids shot open and she grabbed her leg. "Ow! That burns."

"Good. You're awake. Stay that way."

Zain grabbed his phone and tapped the screen.

"Who are you calling?" Carli asked, still clutching her leg.

"Dr. Frye. Sometimes she does house calls for me, on the side."

"Of course she does." Carli cut her eyes at him.

"What's that supposed to mean?"

"She likes you."

"Don't be absurd. She's a doctor and wants to help."

She dabbed the towels at the side of her leg. "Please. No doctor makes house calls anymore unless there's something in it for her. In fact, is there any woman in this town who doesn't have a crush on you? I thought Heather was going to tackle you to the floor when I stopped by the coffee shop yesterday."

Dr. Frye's voice mail picked up. Zain hit the end key and ignored Carli's questions. The last thing he wanted to discuss was Heather. They'd dated a few times after Carli split town, but he wasn't ready for any kind of commitment.

Heather said she understood when he presented the friend card, but the woman had always hoped for more. The way she flirted with him every morning in the coffee shop was a bit desperate. Now, with Carli's return, Heather seemed to be more intense.

"Are you not going to answer me?"

"Nope." The wound still had some dirt around the edges. He poured more water onto her leg.

Carli tensed and sucked in an agonizing breath. "Fine. I'll stop asking about your love life. Just no more irrigation. The wound is clean enough."

He smirked and tapped Candyce's number again.

The doctor picked up. "Zain. It's four a.m. This better be important."

"Carli Moore's been shot, looks like a flesh wound, but she needs stitches and probably an IV."

"Where are you?" Candyce asked.

"Carli's house."

"I'm on my way."

He ended the call and faced Carli. Sweat beaded across her forehead, while the pain robbed her cheeks of their natural pink hue. The bleeding had tapered, but still needed some pressure. He grabbed a clean bandage and wrap.

Carli forced a small smile to her face. "Dr. Candyce to the rescue?"

"She's on her way. Until she gets here, a bandage and wrap will help with the bleeding. Can you put the sole of your foot back on the ottoman to lift up your thigh?"

Her fingers gripped the side of the couch, as she lifted her leg. Grimaced agony swept across her pretty face, and Zain placed the nonstick bandages to the area, then circled her thigh with the wrap. Maybe talking about something else would ease the physical discomfort from her mind.

"Remember when we were teenagers and used to lie on the roof of the old barn to watch the fireworks at your parents' New Year's Eve cookout?"

She straightened her leg a bit. "Yeah. Dad always invited the entire town for his 'festival of lights.' Mom would spend all day fixing her famous chili and cornbread to give out."

"His fireworks show was the best around."

She closed her eyes. "I doubt anyone from the town would come if Tyler and I had the party."

"I'd come."

She inserted her fingers into the palm of his hand and squeezed. "That's because you're a kind, forgiving man. Not many like you left."

This conversation was headed into an area of painful memories. If he was going to get over Carli Moore, then he needed to change the subject. "By the way, the medical examiner told me a few things about the body found in the cave."

Carli pushed with her good leg and tried to sit up a bit more. "What did he say?"

"The dental work matched the records I'd provided from Sadie. She was killed with blunt force trauma to the head. Also, they found a couple of Hot Red gum wrappers in the pocket of your pink sweater."

"That's pretty specific."

"Yeah. Especially since Sadie was allergic to cinnamon. She wouldn't get near the stuff. Can you remember anything else from the night of the party? I know it's fuzzy, but even the smallest detail, like who gave her the gum, might help."

"You think someone gave her the gum?"

"Why else would she have cinnamon gum wrappers in her pocket? If she'd had a choice, she would've gone with mint."

"All I remember is what I told you yesterday in the barn. I wish I could remember more."

So did he, but if she was drugged, she might never remember the details. What-ifs plagued his mind daily. "Anybody with you?"

Carli squinted her eyes closed, like she was trying to return to the scene.

"She did give me some gum. Burned my tongue, probably cinnamon. Told me it would help mask the smell of alcohol. She was afraid Tyler would be upset if he thought I'd been drinking, even though I was drugged. I guess Sadie didn't know that either."

The doorbell rang. "That'll be Candyce. Keep thinking. Maybe more will come back."

Zain stepped from the great room, into the large vaulted foyer, and swung open the door. Candyce stood in front of him, dressed in black yoga gear with her backpack in hand. Her dark hair was swept into a knot on her head. "Got here as fast as I could," she said.

He motioned her inside. "Thanks. Carli's on the couch in the great room."

"You wanna tell me what's going on? How'd she get shot?"

"Long story. I did my best to patch her up, but I think she needs stitches and maybe an IV."

The doctor followed him into the great room. When she saw Carli, she rushed to the couch and retrieved a bag of saline from her backpack.

"You should've called me sooner, Zain. Her pallor doesn't look good." She placed a hand to her wrist and put the stethoscope to Carli's chest. "Any fever or chills?"

"Nothing other than my leg's killing me."

Candyce wrapped a blood pressure cuff tight around Carli's arm. "On a scale from one to ten, how would you describe the pain?"

"About a seven."

Dr. Frye punctured Carli's forearm and inserted the IV catheter, then attached the saline bag tubing. She motioned for Zain. "Hang this on the floor lamp."

Zain did as he was told, while Candyce pulled out a vial of medicine and drew up a syringe. "Carli, I'm going to give you some hydrocodone to help with the pain."

Carli held up her hand. "No, thanks. I'll suffer

through with over-the-counter drugs. Prescription meds make me feel too loopy and I've got a five-year-old to manage."

"Fine." Candyce recapped the unused syringe and placed it back in her bag. "However, it might be good to let Marta handle Eli for a couple of days. You're pale and weak. I'm going to clean the wound, stitch you up and then rewrap the area. You'll want to rest and keep plenty of these antibiotics in your system."

Candyce placed a gold pill bottle in her hand.

"What time is it anyway?" Carli asked.

"Four forty-five a.m."

"Thanks for coming to take care of me. I'm grateful. Most people in this town would've let me rot in the woods."

Zain flinched at the thought, but Candyce didn't miss a beat. She retrieved her medical scissors and began to cut away the bandage he'd applied earlier. Blood had already soaked through.

"There are more folks in this town that would help you, if you let them." Candyce removed a different syringe from a case. "This is some numbing medicine and might hurt a bit."

Zain took a seat and reached for Carli's hand. She squeezed his fingers tight as the agent was injected into her leg. He'd give anything to trade places with her, take the pain on himself. He hated seeing her injured.

"There, the pain should fade for a while."

Comfort spread across Carli's face. Must be nice to feel no pain. If only there was some anesthesia to dull the heartache from his past. One day, he'd have peace when his sister's killer was behind bars.

Candyce kept her hand steady and placed the stitches close together. Her skills were sharp. No wonder she and Sadie had hit it off.

Zain moved the lamp closer for better lighting. "Did my sister ever help you with house calls?"

Candyce glanced at him then steadied her hand again for another stitch. "Sometimes. Sadie loved going into the homes and visiting the patients. When they needed something, like their medicine, I could always count on your sister to take the supplies to them. She was the sweetest person. Our office isn't the same without her."

His sister loved being a nurse. Probably took care of each one of Dr. Frye's patients like she'd cared for Mom. Always right by her side bringing her anything she needed. Zain's phone vibrated and he pulled his hand from Carli's to answer the device. Another text message. He swiped the screen.

Carli's to blame for Sadie's death. I'll make her pay.

Zain pressed up from his seat and moved to the window. The danger wasn't over.

A link popped up underneath the text. A video. He hit the play button with his thumb and lowered the volume. The screen framed Carli struggling to stand while Sadie helped her into her car. This was the night of the party. No way she'd be this out of it from one spiked drink. The drugs must've taken effect quickly.

The video stopped with his sister's face frozen on the screen. A slight smile on her lips. The last image of his sister alive.

"There. All done." Candyce cut the last stitch and cleaned her instruments before returning them to her bag. She checked Carli's vital signs one more time and then faced Zain.

"Walk me out?"

"Sure." He placed a hand on Carli's head. "I'll be right back."

She gave a slight nod and already had her eyes closed. Rest was what she needed now. He followed Candyce onto the porch where she pivoted on her heel toward him.

"Are you going to tell me what happened tonight or do I have to read about it in the papers?"

Zain didn't like letting details out about an ongoing case. He had to be skeptical of everyone. But Dr. Frye was an upstanding citizen in the town. She'd proven herself to be kind and concerned for all the people in their community.

"Carli had an intruder on her property tonight.

When we tried to catch him, he fired a shot, grazing Carli's leg. I really appreciate you coming and taking a look at her."

Candyce grimaced and unzipped her backpack again. "When the drip runs out, she should be good and you can remove the IV from her arm. Here." She handed him two amber pill bottles. "Give her these as directed if she has any pain."

"I thought she said she didn't want any prescription meds."

"She did, but when she wakes up in a few hours and the numbness has faded, she's going to want something stronger than ibuprofen." She turned the other bottle for him to view the label. "This one's for any anxiety. In case she has any post-traumatic stress later from the trauma."

Zain put them in his pocket, but he wasn't going to force anything on Carli that she refused to take. "I really appreciate you coming out this early in the morning."

Her hand fell to his arm with a squeeze. "I'm happy to help. If she develops a fever or red streaks up her leg, then you need to get her to the hospital."

"I can do that."

Candyce glanced at the time on her phone. "Might as well go to the hospital and get my early rounds completed, then head to my office. I have a busy schedule this week, but bring Carli by in a few days. I want to check on her stitches and make sure she's healing well."

"Will do."

She dug through her bag for her keys and Zain noticed a cinnamon pack of gum in the side pocket. The markings looked like the Hot Red brand found with Sadie's remains. He pointed to it. "Mind if I have a piece?"

Candyce glanced at him and then handed him the pack. "Keep it. I've got a full supply at my office."

Zain unwrapped a piece and popped it into his mouth. Definitely cinnamon and strong. Sadie would've stayed as far away from this flavor as possible. "Do you provide this Hot Red gum to your patients?"

Candyce slipped the stethoscope from her neck and placed it in the bag. "Whoever wants it can have some."

Finally, another suspect pool to investigate, and Dr. Candyce Frye was first on Zain's list.

Pain shot through Carli's leg when she bolted up in bed, her nightshirt drenched in sweat. She stared at every shadow in the corners of her room. Figures faded in and out of her vision.

They weren't real. Only a figment of her imagination, the stress of her trauma transforming into the shape of a nightmare. At least that's what

Dr. Frye told her when Carli called two days after the shooting, complaining of insomnia.

She closed her eyes tight and tried to forget the dark figure underneath the bridge, but instead the memory of gunfire flashed toward her again.

Carli pushed the covers off, stood on her good leg and reached for the crutch Zain had dug out of his closet from an old sports injury in college.

Maybe a drink of water would help her get back to sleep. Carli hobbled to the bathroom glancing at the clock on her nightstand as she passed. 5:30 a.m. If her body didn't get back into a normal routine of sleeping until seven, then the dark circles under her eyes would become a permanent fixture on her face.

Carli filled her glass and gulped down the cool liquid. Might as well wash her hair and get ready for the day. Zain would be taking her to her doctor's appointment in a couple hours.

At first, she resisted his offer but since she struggled to press the gas pedal in the truck, she conceded. Marta agreed to watch Eli since the doctor's office was no place for a small child. She rinsed off as best she could without a full-blown shower, doctor's orders for one more day, then dressed and headed downstairs to make some coffee.

She stepped into the kitchen and flicked on

the light. A man's figure stood at the window. Carli screamed.

He turned and faced her. Zain waved from his temporary residence on the sun porch and then entered.

Carli clutched her chest and tried to calm her fight-or-flight response.

"You scared me to death."

"Aren't you used to men peeking in your windows by now?"

Carli hobbled over to the coffee counter and realized the coffee had already been made. "Not particularly. Did you make coffee?"

"Yeah. Couldn't sleep. Did you know your porch has an amazing view of the sunrise over the creek? Woke me up, so I decided to have my first cup of joe with a view. Plus, I decided to go check on my mom. She's an earlier riser than me."

"How's she doing? Still weak?"

"A little better every day. Dr. Frye doesn't think she will ever be back to her pre-cancer self, but she should continue to get stronger."

"That's good."

Carli poured her beverage into a to-go cup, then refilled Zain's. He flashed his knee-weakening smile, with dimples on full display. She could certainly get used to seeing him every morning. "Can I join you for that sunrise view?"

"Sure, but it's starting to fade," he said and opened the screen door onto the porch. Fog drifted across the pastureland and settled over the creek. Steam rose from both their cups as they settled on the cushioned chairs. She sat close to him, the warmth of his body pressed against her shoulder. How she wished he'd wrap an arm around her or try to kiss her again like he'd tried the other night. But that would only complicate matters and wasn't what either of them needed.

Carli lifted her eyes to the sky. Reds, pinks and yellows painted the horizon while birds chirped morning songs to their Maker.

Her vanilla-flavored coffee topped off the warmth in her soul. "Really is beautiful."

She turned her eyes on Zain, who soaked in the landscape.

"Nothing better than God's country." He rubbed the back of his neck and stood. "Your appointment is in thirty minutes. We better get going."

"Sounds good."

Carli deposited their mugs into the sink, then exited to the yard where Zain's SUV was parked. He opened the door for her. A loud snap cracked the morning air. Carli ducked. Her eyes darted across the field then back to the tree line.

Her heart hammered and knocked inside her chest. "What was that?"

Zain pressed against the door. "Sorry. The hinges need some oiling. Every time the door opens, it sounds like those fire poppers kids throw on the Fourth of July."

She climbed into the seat, reached for the handle with shaky fingers and pulled it closed. Zain rounded the front, then slid into the driver's seat. "Are you okay?"

"I guess I'm a little paranoid after being shot. I thought I was doing okay, but lately I've been having trouble sleeping."

"Might want to mention that to Dr. Frye. She can give you some tips to help with getting a good night's rest."

"Says the man who was awake at five thirty in the morning. Maybe you need to follow her tips too."

Zain ignored her comment, started the truck and headed toward town.

A familiar tension rose within her as pastureland turned into tree-lined streets with painted houses, and painted houses turned into shop buildings on Main Street. Every cheerful storefront meant to welcome tourists scolded her presence.

Carli glanced in her passenger-side mirror as Zain turned onto the main road. A dark gray van pulled out behind them. Where'd it come from?

Zain made another turn onto Orchard Street. The van rounded the same bend.

"Do you recognize the vehicle behind us?" she asked Zain.

He glanced in his rearview mirror. "No. Why?"

"They've been following us for the last two turns. Looks like the same van from the bridge the other night, right?"

"I'm not sure. It was dark and I didn't get a good look."

Carli tried to get a better view of the inhabitants. "I can't get a good look at the driver's face."

Zain whipped into a parking space in front of a small convenience store. "Let's see what they do now."

She slid down a bit in her seat and prayed for safety. The scenario playing in her mind was scary enough to be a part of the latest blockbuster action film.

Instead, the van slowed a little when it passed, then drove on by. An older lady with glasses was in the driver's seat and pulled into a parking space several storefronts down at a local diner.

Carli pressed a hand to her chest. Her heart was racing. She raised into a full sitting position and avoided Zain's heavy gaze penetrating her peripheral vision.

He shook his head with a chuckle.

"What?" she asked, a little annoyed at his amusement.

"Nothing. Nothing at all."

He put his truck in Reverse and pulled back on the main road. "Time to get you to the doctor."

They pulled into the parking lot and entered the office of Candyce Frye, located a few stores down from Heather's Coffee Bar. Modern furniture decorated the interior. Zain waited for Carli to check in then helped her find a seat in the busy waiting room. Dr. Frye really did like to start her day early. 7:00 a.m. and the place was already packed.

Some patients coughed, while others were there for a checkup, young and old alike. Zain pointed out two seats with a decent vantage point of everyone present in the room.

Carli shrugged her shoulders out of her jacket. "Is it hot in here to you?"

"A little, maybe."

"I'm burning up. You're coming with me into the exam room with Candyce, right?"

"I can if you want me to."

"I'd feel much safer if you were there."

A young girl dressed in scrubs entered and glanced at the name on her iPad. "Carli Moore."

Zain handed Carli her crutch and escorted her to the patient rooms in the back. Nurses buzzed around the central clinical area gathering supplies for their patients or placing notes in charts.

A blonde girl with bright blue eyes smiled as they approached.

"Hi, Sergeant Wescott. What are you doing here?"

Her name badge read Julia Adams. She was one of Sadie's good friends. His sister bragged on what a brilliant nurse she was.

"I'm here with…" He glanced at Carli and she continued to hobble inside the patient room. "With Carli."

"Is she seeing Dr. Frye today?"

"Yeah."

Zain leaned on the countertop and glanced around at the articles on her desk. Cop habit.

Julia had a cell phone, computer, iPad and unscented hand lotion all placed within easy reach. But one more item caught his attention. A pack of Hot Red gum.

He pointed at the item. "What kind of gum is that? I don't think I've seen the brand in my grocery store."

Julia pulled out a stick and handed it to him. "It's Hot Red. My favorite. Cinnamon flavored. Here, you can have a piece."

He took the item and popped it into his mouth. Time to find out who knew about Sadie's allergy. "Thanks. I bet my sister really liked this flavor."

"Not hardly. She was allergic to cinnamon. I'm surprised you didn't know that."

"That's right. Must've slipped my mind." Zain pointed at another nurses' station nearby that held several packs of Hot Red. "Does Dr. Frye special order the gum for the entire office?"

"She sure does. Her little gift to her employees. I think she doesn't want us to have bad breath when we're with our patients."

Julia grabbed a couple of supplies and headed toward Carli's room. Zain followed. "That's really nice of her. Has she always done that for her staff?"

"As long as I've been here, and that's been at least five years now."

They both stopped outside Carli's door.

Julia grabbed the handle and faced him. "You're not going inside, are you?"

"Actually, Carli requested I come in with her."

She started to protest when something crashed inside.

Julia's eyes widened and she entered the room. Zain followed.

Carli was sitting on the floor, curled into a ball. A metal tray nearby was tipped onto the tiles. Zain rushed to Carli's side.

"Are you okay?"

Fear flashed in her eyes. "There was a man."

"In the room?"

Carli clutched her chest and tried to take in a breath. "No. Outside the window."

Julia placed a stethoscope to Carli's chest. "My name's Julia and I'm a nurse here. You look a little pale. Can you tell me what you're feeling right now?"

"I'm struggling to breathe. Like someone's sitting on my chest."

Zain grabbed a chair and moved it closer, then helped Julia lift Carli to the seat. "I can assure you there's plenty of oxygen in this room for all of us, and we need to slow your breathing. Big deep breaths." Julia kept the listening device in place. "What made you start feeling this way?" the nurse asked.

Carli pointed toward the window. "I saw someone there. A man peering inside. He startled me and I jumped from the bed into the metal tray."

"What did he look like?" Zain asked.

"Tall, muscular, the same build as the man who shot me. He was wearing a mask."

Zain looked at Julia. "Do you have any security guards on-site?"

"We've got one. Joe Capitano." Julia pressed a red call button on the wall and another girl entered. "Go get Joe."

Zain stepped forward before she left. "Tell him to do a search of the grounds. Make sure no men are lurking outside."

Carli's breathing turned rapid again. Her hand

patted her chest. Julia helped her stand and pace the floor of the room. "Walking will help."

"He had a gun. I thought he was going to shoot me right through the window." She bent forward. "Why can't I breathe?"

Zain moved in front of her and took her hands in his. He hated seeing her so scared. "I think you're having a panic attack."

The door opened and Candyce entered. With one look at Carli, she moved into action. "I need you to take a seat on the table."

Zain helped her climb up, and Candyce placed the metal part of the stethoscope to her back and listened, then she flashed a light into her eyes. "Still having trouble breathing?"

Carli nodded.

Candyce turned to Julia. "Let's get two liters of oxygen."

Candyce pulled open a drawer with predrawn syringes and grabbed an alcohol swab. "I'm going to give you some medicine to help calm you down. How many times has this been happening a day?"

"A couple of times. Mostly at night."

Candyce turned to Zain. "Did you not give her the anxiety meds I prescribed?"

"She said she didn't want any prescriptions."

Dr. Frye pressed her lips into a thin line, swiped Carli's arm with an alcohol swab and stuck her with the needle. Zain placed a hand on the doctor's arm.

"What did you give her?"

"A minimal dose of diazepam to calm her down while she's in the office. It's temporary and will wear off in a few hours."

In a few minutes, Carli began to relax, and he helped her rest back on the table. They covered her with a blanket. At least she wasn't shaking anymore.

Security knocked on the door and Zain exited the room to talk to Joe. "Did you see anyone?"

"Not a soul, but on our security cam we caught the edge of a man's black boot near Carli's window. The edge of the building hid most of him, but someone definitely was there."

SEVEN

Carli was starting to feel normal again for the first time since Dr. Frye stitched her up, despite the occasional stab of pain in her leg or rush of panic brought on by nightmares.

Dr. Frye wanted her to come back to the office after her last episode for a follow-up visit today. Probably would ask her a ton of questions. Maybe Carli could dodge a few and convince the doctor to take out her stitches. She scratched at the skin around them. They seemed to be healing.

Zain had been sweet, having coffee with her every morning before going to work. They'd had no more physical contact, but the time they spent together had begun to heal the wounds from their past.

Carli fixed her face and headed to the kitchen for breakfast. The smell of Marta's homemade blueberry muffins rose up the staircase to greet her. Her tummy rumbled, but there was no going faster on the steps with her slight limp. At least she was almost back to her regular gait.

Eli chatted with Marta and seemed eager to eat his breakfast.

"How much longer, Aunt Marta? I'm hungry."

"One more minute, baby. Then we've got to let them cool for two minutes before you can eat them."

Carli rounded the corner. "How many does one plus two make?"

They'd been working on simple addition since Eli would be going to kindergarten next year. His birthday was two weeks after the district's cutoff date and she was thankful she could work with him another year at home. He held up two fingers on one hand and one on the other. His head bobbed with each number.

"Three?"

She ran her fingers over his curls. "You're going to be a whiz in math, little man. I hope Marta has enough for me after you finish eating all of yours, you little bottomless pit of a boy."

Her nephew giggled and dodged away from her tickling hand. "I'm going to eat them all."

Carli stuck out a pouty lip. "But then I won't get any."

"Okay. You can have one."

"Just one?"

"Maybe two, but I'm a growing boy and I need muffins."

Eli licked his lips and rubbed his pooched-out

belly. Marta placed a plate in front of him. "Let's see if you can finish those off first before we put any more on your plate."

He bit into one and smiled with blueberry stain all over his face. "Thanks."

Carli filled up a cup of coffee. "How many of those have you got?"

"Three dozen."

"That's a lot of muffins."

Marta looked at her and smiled. "My mother always told me it is better to have too much food than too little. Therefore, I always bake extra."

"Mind if I take some over to Zain's mom? All this with Sadie's death has been difficult for her. I thought a visit might be nice. It's been a while since I've seen her and to be honest, I've got to get out of this house. I've been cooped up for too long and I'm starting to go stir-crazy."

Marta moved to the cabinet, retrieved a basket and lined it with a cloth. "I think that's a wonderful idea. Go have yourself a nice chat with Ms. Wescott. Tell her I said hello."

"Why don't you come too, Marta? You always did like Ms. Wescott."

"Can I go?" Eli asked.

Carli tousled his hair. "I don't see why not, but not with blueberry stains all over your face. Finish up your muffin and we'll wash off your mouth, then head over in the golf cart."

* * *

Carli lifted her injured leg while Ms. Wescott adjusted the pillow underneath her foot. "Zain told me all about the other night. So scary. I hope they find the guy."

"Me too," Carli said.

"Keep the leg elevated to help with the swelling."

Zain's mother had been a nurse before she was diagnosed with cancer. She worked up until the chemo made her too weak to do her job, but often gave credit to God and her doctors for helping her through the entire ordeal. Probably where Sadie got her medical prowess.

"Thank you. I don't usually make a habit of putting my feet on people's furniture."

The older woman waved a dismissive hand. "Nonsense. If we can't use the furniture, then what good is it?"

Ms. Wescott settled back into her chair next to Marta and took a bite of the muffin. "These are amazing."

Marta smiled. "Thank you."

Carli patted the woman's hand. "No one bakes like Ms. Marta."

"Isn't that the truth. You're blessed to have her."

"Yes, we are. She's been a huge help with Eli, the shooting and everything. She filled such a large void for me after Mother died."

Especially after Carli found out she was adopted.

She was so angry at her parents for keeping the details of her birth parents a secret. Marta helped her realize they did so because they loved her.

"Virginia Moore was an amazing woman. Gave me a job taking care of two beautiful children. She was a friend to me in the worst times of my life," Marta added.

"Yes, she was. Always let Zainy come over and ride horses or tool around the ranch with Carli. Those two couldn't be separated when they were little."

Marta laughed. "I remember. Although I think it was Carli who was always following Zain."

"Maybe so." Ms. Wescott focused on Carli. "Zain was beside himself with worry the other night after the shooting. Blamed himself for allowing you to be in the line of fire. Said he should've made you stay at the house."

Carli shifted in her seat. "Well, that wasn't going to happen. I was determined to go and am thankful God protected us. Things could've been a lot worse."

"Much worse."

Ms. Wescott took another bite of the muffin in her hand. "Mmm. Marta, you must give me the recipe. Let's go into the kitchen and I'll find a pen and paper for you to write down the items I need to purchase."

A smile spread across Marta's face, clearly

flattered someone other than Carli and Tyler bragged on her baking skills. The two women exited the room and Eli slumped back on the couch. "I'm bored, Aunt Carli. Can I go outside and play on the tire swing?"

"We just got here and you're already bored?"

The boy nodded, bouncing his curls. Carli glanced out the window at the deputy stationed on the porch. She hated keeping Eli cooped up inside all the time. The boy loved the outdoors more than the horses. "Fine. But stay in the front yard where Deputy Judd can see you and don't go past the swing, okay?"

"I won't."

The front door closed behind him and Carli's gaze drifted to the stairs leading to the second level. Sadie's bedroom was at the top. Carli hadn't been there since the day her friend disappeared. Tensions had been high between her and Zain before their breakup and Carli spent the afternoon crying on Sadie's bed.

Maybe something inside the room would trigger more of her memories and help Zain find Sadie's killer.

Carli lowered her leg off the pillow with only a flinch of pain, stood and glanced toward the kitchen hallway. The two older women were still out of sight, laughter echoing through the rooms about a funny tidbit. They wouldn't miss her at all.

Wooden stairs creaked with Carli's weight. Zain and his mom lived in an older house, but the bones held such character. Her fingers slid up the hand-carved railing, ending with a swirl right outside of Sadie's room.

Carli kept her eyes focused on the closed door. Pink letters spelled out her best friend's name across the wooden slats. She turned the knob and walked inside.

Everything still sat in the identical place where Sadie left it. Fuzzy pink pillows on her bed. Teddy on her shelf. Even an old photo of the two of them sitting on the barn roof during one of her father's fireworks shows was stuck on the mirror.

Carli retrieved it for a closer look. Sadie wore her butterfly necklace in the photo. The following summer her best friend gave it to her. Said she wanted her to have it to take to Atlanta as a memento. Carli flipped the image over. "Eighty-two" was written on the back. Not sure what the number meant since that was not the year the photo was taken.

Maybe Ms. Wescott wouldn't mind if she kept the picture. She'd ask her when she went back downstairs.

Carli started for the door then stopped. Behind a musical jewelry box, something red caught her eye. She lifted and inspected the object. A pack of gum. Hot Red. Only one piece left.

"What are you doing in here?" Zain's voice bounded behind her. Carli spun around, her hand over her heart. He did not look happy to see her.

"I thought being in Sadie's room again might help me remember something from the night she disappeared."

His grip tightened on the doorknob. "You mean the night she was killed?"

"Yeah," she said, fumbling with the pack of gum in her hand. He seemed tense. Not like his jovial self from the last few times they'd watched the sunrise together on her porch.

He stepped to the side and nodded toward the hallway. "You need to go back downstairs. Mom doesn't like for anyone to be in Sadie's room."

"Then I guess she wouldn't let me keep this photo."

Zain crossed to her in two strides. "No. Leave everything as is. That's the way Mom wants it and that's the least I can give her after all she's been through."

Carli took one last look at the picture and stuck it back in the crack of the mirror. "By the way. Did you see this?"

Zain's gaze fell to the pack of gum in her hand. "Hot Red?"

"Wasn't this the kind of wrapper you found in the sweater pocket on Sadie? There's only one piece left."

"That doesn't mean it's the same pack from the night she disappeared."

"True. But like you said, she's allergic to cinnamon. If not from that night, then when?"

Zain fiddled with the pack, flipping it back and forth in his hands. "She touched this that night."

"Wouldn't have chewed a piece though. Not with her allergies. In fact, I'm surprised she even had it in her room."

Carli wandered to the window overlooking Zain's backyard. The old swimming hole sat at the bottom of the hill. They used to dam the water when they were kids and discuss fun topics other than murder. She almost forgot what it was like to have a normal conversation with him. This tragedy dominated every aspect of their lives.

"How many pieces of gum did Sadie give you that night?" Zain asked, pulling her from the memories.

"I think two."

"I saw a pack of this gum in Dr. Frye's bag the night she came to stitch you up."

Carli faced him. "She chews the same kind of gum found on Sadie's remains? Did you question her?"

"Not yet, but I've got someone tailing her. Of course, she provides this flavor for the entire office, which opens up a whole pool of suspects other than your brother."

"Did you tell Lieutenant Black? With the texts and this, if you go to him and share what you've discovered, then he'll leave Tyler alone when he gets back."

"It's still not enough."

How could Zain think that? The higher-ups at the sheriff's office must be so stubborn if they were unwilling to consider new evidence that proved her brother's innocence. "Not enough? It's plenty to create doubt and get them looking at other suspects."

Zain took a seat on the end of the bed. "I'm not even supposed to be working Sadie's case. If they find out and put me on desk duty, then I'm not free to follow the leads or to protect you and Eli. That's not a risk I'm willing to take until I can prove who's doing this."

Carli snatched the gum pack from his hand. "I can't believe you are going to step away from helping my brother. I should've known. You still think he's guilty, don't you?"

"No, I don't, but—"

"Oh please. You're scared of losing your job and are willing to sacrifice my brother's freedom to keep your badge." She pushed past him. "Fine then. I'll talk to them. Tell them they've got the wrong man. Let's see what they say about that."

EIGHT

Zain followed Carli down the stairs and out his front door, which she released in time to slam against him. He had to stop her from going to Lieutenant Black. If Tyler ever chewed the Hot Red gum, then it would only put more ammo in the prosecution's case.

He stepped outside and leaned against the porch railing. Carli stood on the sidewalk leading to the driveway and motioned to her nephew. "Eli, let's go!"

"Carli, wait."

She spun on her heel at the bottom of the porch steps and faced him, narrowed eyes blazing with anger. "I can't believe you of all people, would put your career before a human being's freedom. What happened to you? Maybe your crush on Dr. Frye is skewing your objectivity."

"First off, I don't have a crush on Candyce. Second, if your brother ever chewed Hot Red gum, then the prosecution will use what you're about to give them against your brother. Going to them could hurt him."

She hesitated for a moment and blinked at the last bit of information. He hoped he'd convinced her to wait. "I want to help you, Carli. And your brother. But you've got to trust me on this."

Trust didn't come easy for either one of them. Not after their breakup.

Zain's mom stepped out on the porch with Marta behind her. "What's all the yelling about?"

He held up his hand. The last thing he wanted to do was drag his mother into their argument. "Nothing Carli and I can't work out, Mom."

Carli motioned to her nanny. "Marta, it's time to go."

"What? Why so soon?"

Carli's gaze focused back on him. "I just need to leave."

Ms. Wescott descended the stairs and stood between the two of them. "Zain, what did you do?"

He kept his gaze locked on Carli. "I'm trying to help her."

Carli took a couple of steps closer and tossed him the pack of gum, then walked across his driveway, a slight limp in her gait.

He couldn't let her leave like this without a plan in place. Zain followed her to the golf cart and grasped the front bar. She looked past him toward Eli still playing on the swing. "Eli, let's go."

His next question might make her angrier, but better for him to know now than bring up her brother later. "When will Tyler be home?"

Her green-eyed gaze flashed to his again and she hesitated. He admired her moxie to defend her brother. "Next week. His truck broke down in St. Louis, Missouri, and he's been delayed."

She paused and her hard expression softened. "We have to help him, Zain. If not, then they'll question him again now that they found her body on our property. He doesn't deserve that."

"I know. When he gets home, have him call me first. We'll put a plan together. And get ahold of that bulldog lawyer of yours. We might need him."

Zain ducked his head down and waved at Eli and Marta. "Thanks for baking muffins for my mom. She loves having company come by. Keeps her from being bored."

Carli shifted the cart into gear, but kept her foot on the brake. "By the way, there was a number on the back of the photo of me and Sadie. Eighty-two. Mean anything to you?"

Zain shook his head. "No, nothing at all."

Carli nodded and picked up her phone. The same text with a video link he received a week ago appeared on her screen. "I wouldn't watch that if I were you," Zain said.

"Why?"

"It's a video from the night Sadie went missing posted on her social media page. Someone sent it to me the night you were shot. Not something you want to see, trust me."

Carli tucked the device into her back pocket. "Trusting you is something I'm struggling with these days."

Another blow to his ego, as she backed out of the driveway.

Zain moved to his front porch. His mother stood at the top with her hands on her hips. "What is it with you and Carli Moore? I've never seen so much pent-up tension between two people in my life. Why don't you tell the girl you love her and get on with it?"

He joined her and took a seat in one of the red rocking chairs. "We have a lot of unresolved issues between us."

"Is that what you call it? Because where I come from, you're smitten, boy. And if you want any kind of future with that girl, it's best not to keep making her mad."

"I'm doing my job, Mom."

She moved into the chair beside him. "Will you be able to help her brother?"

"I hope so. I'm going to try, but it's not going to be easy."

She placed a hand on his chest. "I've never known you to back down from a fight, Zain Wescott, and this one is particularly important."

The screen door creaked when his mother went inside and left him to ponder her words. He needed more evidence and one of the ways to get that was to talk with Tyler.

He lifted his phone and called Dale. Maybe his DEA friend had some luck on finding Carli's brother. "Any news on Tyler?"

"We found him in California, then tracked him to…" A few papers rustled in the background followed by a few clicks with a mouse. "St. Louis, Missouri. He's staying at the Château on the Skye Resort. His truck broke down and he was delayed, but seems to be on track for home."

Zain would have to work fast. By the time Tyler got his truck fixed and drove into town next week, he'd need to be ready with a new suspect and plenty of evidence.

His friend exhaled into the phone. "Listen, I'm not sure how to tell you this, so I'm gonna come right out with the news. It's about your sister."

What more could Dale have uncovered about Sadie? "Sounds serious. What's up?"

Mom stepped back out on the porch. "There's

one more thing I want to say— Oh sorry, I didn't know you were on the phone."

Zain didn't want her to overhear their conversation about Sadie. "Hang on a minute, Dale."

Zain muted the phone and stood. "I've got to go to the office, Mom. Can we talk more tonight when I get home?"

"Of course. I just wanted to say that Carli looks especially pretty these days. I've always liked her."

Zain didn't want to encourage his mother's matchmaking. Instead of responding, he gave her a kiss on the cheek, moved across the yard and climbed into his truck. With the door closed and air-conditioning running, he unmuted his friend. "Sorry about that. What did you find on my sister and why are you even looking into her?"

"She popped up in the DEA case I'm working. After you called the other night and told me about finding her remains, I uploaded her autopsy report into our system and got an alert. I'm not sure how to tell you this, man, but Sadie's DNA was found at one of the drug busts we conducted a few years ago."

"That's impossible."

"Not according to our records. I'll send you a digital copy of the report."

"When was this?"

"Two years ago, in June."

Sadie disappeared three months later, in September. She'd barely been back from her three-month internship Dr. Frye arranged in Charlotte at the trauma center there. "There must be a mistake."

"No mistake. The house we entered had her blood in one of the bedrooms. The evidence never matched anyone in our system until I accessed her autopsy report the other day. Our customized algorithm matched the two documents together. We think her death must've had something to do with the case."

Sadie came home that August looking more tired than usual, but went back to work at Dr. Frye's right away. He figured it was because she'd been busy with her internship. Zain tried to absorb the information. What would Sadie be doing at a drug bust?

"Zain? You there?"

"Yeah." He raked a hand through his hair. "I need to look into what you've told me about Sadie. I can go back over some records we have on file detailing her movements the last few weeks before her death. Maybe I can get a better handle on this new information."

"Sounds good."

Zain pulled out of his drive with Sadie on his mind. How did his sister's blood end up at one of Dale's drug busts? He needed to go back over the autopsy report himself and compare it to the documents Dale planned to send.

Before he headed back to the office, he wanted to take another look around the covered bridge on Carli's property. He'd sent a team to search and they came back with tire tracks, bullet casings from the shooting and one boot print. They were moving forward, but he needed more. He had less than a week.

A red gabled roof welcomed him as he rounded the curve in the road to the small bridge on Carli's property. The sides were open with poured concrete for the base. The babble of Crystal Creek ran underneath the structure.

If only he were here to relax, have a picnic on the banks, like he and Carli used to do, but instead Zain grabbed a shovel from his truck toolbox, shuffled underneath and climbed to the abutment where the intruder had been digging.

His shovel sliced into the fresh dirt and sand covering the area. He dug in several places with no luck. Then with one deep slice, a clang echoed within the hole. A few more transfers and Zain removed a metal box.

His hand brushed debris from the lid. No markings were on the outside. He unlatched the clasp and opened the box. Empty prescription pill bottles filled the space. Zain lifted and rotated one to view the white sticker on the front.

Fentanyl was the opioid prescribed, but another detail disturbed him more than the drug.

Sadie's name was listed on every bottle.

Zain had never known Sadie to take any pills. She gave them to her patients, made sure their mother took her meds, but Sadie preferred natural remedies to treat herself. Clearly, his sister was involved in more trouble than he ever realized.

"What did you get yourself into, Sadie Mae?"

Carli snuggled into the couch, propped her leg on a pillow and stared at the video link. What could be bad enough for Zain to discourage her from watching? She'd experienced the night of Sadie's death and regretted her actions every day since. Maybe the footage would trigger a memory and she could finally bring some assistance to finding Sadie's killer.

Her thumb pressed the link.

Sadie's social media page opened. The screen displayed her friend's face with a button in the middle. Carli pressed Play.

Loud yelling emitted from her phone speakers and Carli fumbled to hit Pause, then cut the volume down. She didn't want to wake Eli from his nap.

Her finger tapped the large play arrow in the middle of the screen again, and she focused on the details. Sadie's face filled her view. She had her arm wrapped around Carli's waist and waved a dismissive hand at the camera person.

"Put that away. The last thing we need is a recording of this."

Her friend's voice held the same sweet concern she had for all her patients.

The videographer ignored her request and continued to film. This was the night of the party.

Carli hoped to hear a voice, something to help her figure out who was with Sadie that night. Several guys and girls from their town danced or laughed behind her at the bonfire. Some roasted marshmallows or hot dogs. Some taunted Carli for her compromised state.

Sadie moved her away from the group. Probably toward the car and into the back seat. She closed the door and then put her hand over the camera, pushing the aim toward the ground. The tips of the person's shoes flashed on the screen before everything went black.

Carli ran back a few frames. Black, nondescript boots. Definitely large, man-sized. Who would be with her best friend?

Sadie wasn't dating anyone at the time. At least no one she'd divulged to Carli, and they talked about everything. She'd never mentioned having a boyfriend, although many men in town flirted with Sadie, but the beautiful blond-haired, blue-eyed girl seemed to be holding out for someone better. Someone who could match her sass and wit.

Carli scrolled through the comments. Hateful words filled the space. Most aimed at Carli. Many blamed her or her brother for Sadie's death.

Maybe someone should put her and her brother in the cave.

Another wrote,

Probably planned her murder together. They should be pushed out of town and shot.

Tears salted her couch pillow as she continued to read at least thirty negative comments. Then they stopped. After one supportive comment.

He without sin, cast the first stone.

Carli stared at the posted name. Dr. Candyce Frye.

Carli made a mental note to thank the kind woman when she saw her again.

Footsteps shuffled into the room. "What's the matter? Why are you crying?" Marta asked.

She pushed into a sitting position on the couch,

letting Marta take the seat beside her. "The whole town hates me."

"That's not true."

"Here, look at this."

Carli handed her the phone and watched the woman's face tighten with each scroll. She placed the device on the coffee table and took Carli's hands.

"My dear girl, you've dealt with far greater grief than this. You're strong. You've survived the death of your parents and sister-in-law, the death of your best friend, and made a successful life for yourself. You will get through this also." Marta brushed a stray hair from Carli's face. "I'm proud of you."

"All the comments hurt, ya know?"

"I know, but I'm going to tell you what I told my niece when she was having some problems at work with her colleagues. You were not made to please man. You were created and put on this earth to bring glory to God. To love Him. His beauty, His goodness and His love are in you. We are created in His image for a purpose. Now what do you think that purpose might be?"

Carli ran her fingers through her hair. "Right now, to help Zain find Sadie's killer and clear our family name."

"And?"

"To keep Eli safe. At least while I'm here."

"Then that's what you need to focus on. Not a bunch of idiot comments that surfaced on the internet. Besides, by tomorrow there will be a new victim being attacked on social media and all of this will be forgotten."

"I wouldn't wish cyberbullying on anyone."

Marta patted her hand. "That's because you have a good heart and all these other people don't. Now, how about a hot tea to make you feel better."

"Sounds good. Thank you, Marta."

The familiar clang of glasses and kitchen noises calmed Carli. Marta always had a way of putting everything in perspective. Probably because the woman trusted God more than anyone else Carli knew. Her heart was kind. A woman to model.

"Marta, I'll be back in a minute."

"Don't you want your tea?"

"I'll drink it when I get back. Will you check on Eli for me?"

"When he wakes up from his nap, I need to run to the store. You mind if I take him with me?"

"Not at all." Carli grabbed her phone and keys then headed for the truck. The pain from her wound was minimal since Dr. Frye had removed her stitches today after she'd left Zain's house. She didn't want to think about him right now.

Carli replayed the video.

In it, Sadie's car was parked right by the barn. She could've met someone there, like they thought before. Maybe something at the old barn site would help her remember. If she was going to fulfill her purpose while she was here, then she needed to work harder.

She bounced her truck down the dirt road and pulled inside the wide-open barn door, letting the shade cool her.

With a push of her sunglasses onto her head, Carli grabbed her gun and stepped from the vehicle. She probably didn't need a weapon, but after all the turmoil lately, she wanted to be safe, and the boot prints imprinted into the ground next to hers didn't bring much comfort.

Carli squatted and took a closer look. Maybe a size thirteen with definitive tread marks. She took a photo and stepped across to keep them intact. Someone had been here recently.

But why?

Carli's brother stored hay and old farm equipment inside, but spent most of his time with the horses in the new facility about fifty yards away. This boot print was fresh. The imprint couldn't be Tyler's. His foot was smaller. Had the person who shot her been in the barn before heading to the bridge that night?

She moved into the second stall. The first one was filled with equipment.

Boards above her squeaked.

Carli stopped.

Her pulse increased, pounding inside her ears. Wind whipped through the cracks and crevices of the structure. Probably old boards stretching to allow a breeze to pass through.

Her paranoia had been on high alert since she'd been shot. Never could be too careful. Her hand tightened on the grip of her weapon and she tried to refocus. Look for anything out of the ordinary.

Movement brushed through her periphery. Carli spun on her heel and raised her gun.

A small golden-haired kitten jumped down from the ledge and rubbed against her leg. Sunlight from the window behind Carli bathed the barn cat in an afternoon hue.

She dropped her arm and leaned against the back stall door leading outside. "You scared me, silly cat."

The furry animal made a figure eight, crossing between her legs. A slight purr emanated from deep inside its little body.

Carli squatted to pet the animal.

A loud bang echoed in the space.

Glass shattered over her.

Carli dove behind the interior sliding stall door

while the kitten darted through a small hole outside to safety. Another shot rang through, the bullet barely missing her head.

Boards on the outside wall splintered when two more bullets hit.

If she stood, then her life would be over. The shooter must be in the loft area above her. She was a sitting duck.

Carli moved to the edge and fired back.

A scuffle clamored on the second floor.

She ran, pushed open the back stall door and rolled into the field.

Outside the barn, she moved to the corner. Maybe they'd follow her and she could double back. Slip inside the front of the barn and get the truck.

Wind whipped her hair into her eyes.

Thunder boomed overhead and dark clouds rolled.

If she didn't hurry, gunfire might not be the only thing to threaten her life.

From the looks of the impending storm, she didn't want to be outside much longer. Lightning loved striking the tallest objects in an open field.

She scanned the acreage. The same black van from the night at the bridge sat against the tree line, empty.

Carli needed to get to the truck.

She ran inside the first-stall door and pressed

her body against the wall. Large pieces of farm equipment blocked her path to the main aisle.

Box scrapes, blades, plows and mowers filled the space in front of her. Not the easiest path to her vehicle. She'd have to crawl over.

Something thumped in the stall next to her and shadows tripped the light beams shining through.

Carli peered between the wooden slats of the wall between them. Male, dark headed and muscular. Same build as the man who shot her last week. She couldn't see his face. He headed for the stall's back exit.

If she didn't get to the truck now, he'd find her. Carli began climbing over green obstacles, trying to keep her footsteps from clanging on the metal. Over, under, around…all to get closer to her only path of escape.

She reached the interior stall door. A glint of metal in the dirt caught her eye. She reached down and lifted a chain from the ground. Unique and intricate, like the one she wore around her neck, but no locket.

More shots pinged around her.

Carli ducked and ran, hopping into the driver's seat of the truck.

With a quick start, she hit the gas and plowed out the end of the barn, near the creek. A glance in her rearview mirror displayed the man exiting, gun raised. Still too far away to get a good look at his face.

Carli headed toward the house. She needed more ammunition and hopefully Marta and Eli would be gone to the store. Tyler's bedroom safe held all his gun paraphernalia. Her feet hit the front steps and she plowed up to her brother's bedroom.

Carli grabbed an extra revolver from the nightstand drawer and moved into the closet. Only two clips for her Glock and one box of shells at her disposal.

She closed the door and pulled out her phone.

"911. What's your emergency?"

"There's an intruder on our property."

"Is he in the house?"

"Not yet. He shot at me a couple of times in the barn."

Carli rummaged through a couple of her brother's travel bags for a pair of earbuds. He was always going on trips. Surely, he had a set. She needed her hands free, but didn't want to put the female operator on speaker. Her fingers dug into the front pocket of one of his duffels and discovered the listening device. She put one bud in her ear and let the other hang. Still no noises from downstairs.

"What's your address?"

"153 Moore Road."

Keys clicked through in the background. "I'm dispatching officers to your premises. Are you in the house or barn?"

"House."

"Where are you located inside the house?"

"I'm in the master bedroom closet."

"Is that upstairs or on the main floor?"

"Upstairs, end of the hall."

"Are you armed?"

"Yes. I have two guns with me. Hurry, please. I'm scared."

"You're doing great, ma'am. Stay on the line with me and we'll be there soon. Officers are fifteen minutes away."

In fifteen minutes, she might be dead if the intruder found her. Carli kept the operator on the line and texted Zain. If he was home, he might be able to arrive before the officers.

NINE

Zain clicked through his sister's files. If his lieutenant found out he was nosing around in the case, he'd be reprimanded for sure. But this was his family and there was no way he was going to sit by without checking out the details. Besides, knowing and interfering were two different things. He wanted to make sure nothing dropped through the cracks this time.

The autopsy report still contained the same information even after his fifth reading. He'd read the same words so many times he could almost recite them from memory.

There had to be something. Anything. Skin under her nails or a fiber on her clothing to point him in the right direction.

"Come on, Sadie. Show me who did this to you."

Zain clicked through the screens. The police report the two deputies submitted from the party that night revealed little other than they broke up the party and sent everyone home. They'd taken down the names of participants, but Sadie's name wasn't listed. Must've already been gone.

If only he'd been the one to break up the party instead of procrastinating, then he could've gone looking for her. Maybe she'd still be alive.

Since that day, he completed his tasks. By the book. No shortcuts. No mistakes. Even some of the recent deputy graduates called him hard-nosed behind his back. He didn't mind. If it saved another life like his sister's, then the teasing would be worth it.

Maybe if he'd been responsible, Sadie's body wouldn't be lying in a cold morgue waiting to be placed in an empty burial plot.

A buzzing vibrated along his desk, but he'd flipped it over so he wouldn't be distracted. He could call them back later.

A knock on his door interrupted his task.

Nate entered and placed a coffee in front of him. "You've had your head down buried in those monitors all day. Did you even eat lunch?"

Zain glanced at his watch and realized the time was three hours past noon. "I guess not."

He lifted his phone and texted his mother an apology for the absence. She'd worry if he didn't show. After losing one child, she was a bit paranoid about knowing his location. He didn't mind. If the knowledge brought her comfort, then that's what mattered. Anything to keep the sad memories of Sadie's death at bay.

"Where are you at? Anything I can do to help?"

"Yeah. Maybe if I walk through this aloud, the two of us can put our heads together. See if anything sticks."

"Sounds good. Hit me."

"Okay. Around midnight, complaints of a noise disturbance issued by Tyler Moore started the events of the evening. Officers arrived on scene around one. They told the attendees to head home after they cleaned up their mess. They all agreed. But Sadie and Carli's names were not listed among the group even though the party was on Carli's land. Do you think they'd already left by then?"

Nate picked up a marker and moved to the whiteboard. "Possibly. When did Tyler say he picked up Carli by the road?"

"Around twelve fifteen." Two hours after their big fight. The one that started the demise of their relationship. Zain wished she'd told him about the adoption, about everything that caused her to doubt their relationship.

He hadn't been happy about her leaving, but they could've figured it out. Things had been going well up until then. He thought they were on the same page. He'd been wrong.

Nate's marker squeaked on the board and drew Zain back to the present. This was not the time to get sentimental.

He lifted his cup to his lips and hoped the dark beverage would somehow trigger a spontaneous revelation in this case. "This reminds me of the old days. Remember?"

"Yeah. I wanted to be a detective and we stayed after our shift, looking up the cold cases to see if we could figure them out."

Zain sank back against his desk and stared at the board, his mind still on Carli. "Thanks, man. I appreciate your help on this. I guess I've been a little too preoccupied with a case that I'm not even supposed to be investigating."

"Preoccupied? More like obsessed."

"Fine. I'm obsessed. But you would be too if you found your sister's dead body in a cave."

"True. I got your back, man. No way I'm telling Lieutenant Black what you do on your days off. Besides, I'd be in trouble too, if he found out how much I share with you about Sadie's case. He'd probably boot us both to desk duty."

"Probably."

A comfortable silence invaded the space between them as they stared at the information. Nate folded his arms across his chest. "Her death isn't our fault you know. You've got to stop punishing yourself for your absence that night."

Zain rubbed the back of his neck, stood and moved to his window. Not the best view in the building, but he could see the edge of town. "I wish I could."

Nate moved to his side. "An evil person took Sadie's life. We're going to find them and that person will be the one who will be guilty of taking her from you. But you need to stop blaming yourself."

"I know, but it's not that easy."

Nate placed a hand on Zain's shoulder and squeezed. "Once we have him behind bars, it'll be easier."

His friend was right. He dreamed of the day he could look Sadie's killer in the eyes, locked in a jail cell. They'd make sure they found him and put him away for the rest of his life.

Nate moved back toward the door. "By the way, there's someone here to see you."

Zain lowered himself into his desk chair again. "Who?"

"Feds."

"Seriously? To work on my sister's case?"

"Afraid so. The lieutenant wants them to talk to—"

"Sergeant Wescott." Two men entered Zain's office and cut off Nate's sentence. "Glad we caught you. I was afraid you'd be gone for the day."

Nate gave a little salute. "And that's my cue to exit."

"I'll catch up with you later."

Lieutenant Maddox Black stepped farther into the room, standing six foot four with an air of respect in his posture. He was a kind, but firm man who followed the letter of the law. A trait Zain admired and implemented since Sadie's disappearance. Black motioned behind him. "I believe you know Special Agent Hunt."

Zain's eyes widened as his friend Dale walked into view. He took his hand and gave him a one-slap hug. "What are you doing here?"

"I came to see you, man."

Unusual for Dale to visit during the day, unless a case was involved. This had to be more than a friendly visit. "Just out of the blue?"

Dale glanced at Lieutenant Black, who gave him a nod. "Not exactly. Truth is, I'm here to take over your case."

Zain's gaze bounced between the two men. Had Dale shared with his lieutenant how much work he'd been doing behind the scenes trying to find Sadie's killer?

"If you're talking about my sister's case, then you should know that case isn't assigned to me. Detective Nate Steele's overseeing the details."

Lieutenant Black pushed his hands into his pockets. "Of course, he is. On paper anyway, and he's doing a fine job. Dale here will explain everything. If you don't mind, I've got another meeting to attend. I'll let you two catch up. Agent Hunt, my door's always open should you need anything."

"Thank you, sir."

Black closed the door behind him and Zain motioned toward a chair for Dale. "Wanna tell me what's going on, fill me in on the case?"

"That's funny. You and I both know you're the most up-to-date person on your sister's murder. How many times have you called asking for tabs on Tyler?"

"You kept that between you and me, right? Not sure Lieutenant Black would be thrilled knowing I had you tailing a private citizen, even if it was on my own time."

"Of course. I'd never tattle like that. What kind of friend would I be to go running to your supervisor degrading your work behind your back?"

"The kind no one trusts. However, there are officers out there who are willing to tear down anyone in an effort to get ahead. Toss ya right under the bus and not think a thing about it."

"Yeah. Those are the kind of guys I stay away from."

"Well, Nate's not one of them. He's one of the best detectives I know."

"True. He sent some of his work on Sadie's

case. Top-notch. Makes my entire job much easier."

"Why exactly did the DEA send you here?"

Dale dropped his gaze and his body posture stiffened. Zain had been reading people for years and this man had information he didn't want to spill.

Perhaps he'd discovered more about Sadie than her DNA matching the blood at an old drug-bust scene. Zain already knew about the pill bottles and had Nate enter them into evidence.

Zain shifted in his seat. He didn't want to believe his sister was involved in something shady, but as more of these puzzle pieces fit together, he couldn't help but wonder what she'd gotten herself into.

Dale tapped his fingertips together, then cleared his throat. "I don't have good news, so I'm going to lay it all out for you."

"Okay. Shoot."

"I told you about Sadie's blood and DNA being found at one of our old drug stings, right?"

"Yeah. I'm still trying to wrap my head around that piece of info. Hard for me to believe my straight A, innocent little sister would've ever been at some seedy DEA bust. I'm wondering if somehow one of your agents got her mixed up with someone else."

Dale retrieved his phone and tapped the screen

a few times. "And that's why cops should never work on their family's cases. We're biased."

Maybe he had a point, but there was no way Zain was going to stay away from his sister's case and if Dale suggested as much as the new manager, Zain would put him in his place.

His friend slid his cell toward him. "We made a positive ID on this video clip one of our guys pulled from a street cam located across the street from our drug bust. Date and time-stamped, two years ago, June 16. The summer before Sadie disappeared."

Zain stared at the footage. Sadie was seen entering an older home and then about thirty minutes later exiting. There had to be some mistake. Sadie would never get mixed up with drugs. She was always the one rescuing her friends after a night of bad judgment.

How then was she in this clip? The quality, clear.

"Did you have any idea about her involvement back then?" Dale asked, his voice softer this time.

Zain racked his memory. Two years ago. That was the time his mother was going through chemo and was in a tremendous amount of pain. Sadie always managed to come up with the funds to pay for medical expenses.

Once, he asked where she was getting the

money. She shrugged it off. Gave some explanation about Dr. Frye helping her with access to some drug programs designed to help patients with cancer.

Was this what she meant? Often the best lies carry a bit of truth to them and if Sadie was dishonest, then he fell for her act.

Zain rubbed his hand on the back of his neck. "Maybe she was there buying pain pills for my mom. The pain was pretty bad back then with her treatments and Sadie wanted to help her."

Dale took in an audible breath then exhaled. "I don't think you understand, Zain. Sadie wasn't there purchasing the drugs. She was there as the dealer."

Silence.

No sounds in the house and no replies from Zain. Where was a good man when a girl needed him?

Carli glanced at her phone. The battery was blinking red and she'd be losing contact with the 911 operator soon. "My phone's about to die. Are the officers close?"

"Five minutes out."

"There's supposed to be a deputy on guard at my house, but he's not here."

"We had to call all units to a burglary in progress. I've got two units on their way."

"I'm going to save what battery I have left and

hang up. I'll try to get to my landline downstairs in the office and call back."

"Can you give me that number?"

She recited the number for the operator.

Carli shut down her phone and darkness enveloped her. Tyler had to have a flashlight somewhere. He'd always kept one hidden when they were kids so he could get up and play with his toys after he was supposed to be in bed. Maybe there was one on the top shelf. Carli stood on her tiptoes, slid her hand across and bumped something hard. Found it. She pulled it down and flicked on the switch. The glow was a bit dim. Probably about dead too. At least her weapon didn't run on batteries.

Carli scooted to the door to listen. Passing time felt like hours, but according to the last look on her phone, ten minutes had passed. Sirens sounded in the distance. If the man in the barn followed her, maybe he'd hear them and think twice about coming inside.

As she leaned against the door frame, something pressed into her arm and she reached for it.

Her fingers grasped the locket on her necklace and slipped the piece of jewelry over her head, holding it under the glow of the flashlight.

Brilliance gleamed in the reflection off the base, highlighting detailed edging. A teal butterfly sat on top, wings lifted into the air, giving it a three-dimensional look.

With a press of the clasp, a small photo inside displayed her and Sadie. Two young women on college graduation day. So much hope in their happy expressions. Best friends ready to take the world by storm. They had planned to make a difference in the health care and marketing worlds.

"Why did you leave me?" She whispered the question, as if the moment was sacred. "Who killed you, Sadie? You've got to help me find the person who took your life."

The locket slipped from her fingers and fell onto the hardwood floor with a clatter. Carli scrambled to retrieve the piece before it rolled into a nook never to be found again. That was the last memento from her friend and she'd never forgive herself if she lost it.

With a quick swipe, Carli uncurled her fingers. The wings of the butterfly were popped up from their original position, synced together. She tried to press them back into place when the body of the creature slid down extending below the base. A slight click secured the extension.

Carli no longer held a locket. Instead, Sadie's butterfly had transformed into a key. Her friend must've had the piece custom-made.

Why would Sadie give her a key before the party on the last night she was alive? Her friend never mentioned any secret journals, lockboxes or safes she had. The necklace now held an ominous meaning, more than just a gift from her friend. Sadie wanted her to find the key and possess whatever knowledge this unlocked. Carli needed to figure out what the key opened, but how?

A thump sounded downstairs.

Carli slipped the jewelry back over her head and hid it beneath her shirt. The intruder wanted the key. That was evident. He'd ransacked her bedroom looking for it and shot at her in the barn when she interrupted his search.

Now he'd followed her inside her house.

Carli picked up her gun, stood, then stepped closer to the door.

The pounding of her heart pulsed in her ears, her breathing grew rapid. He was here. Her attacker. She tightened her grip on her weapon. He might take her life, but she'd put bullet holes in him too.

Seconds passed. Silence.

Maybe it was Zain if he got her text. She grabbed her phone again and hoped she had enough battery to check her messages. Still no response from him. Maybe if she told him someone was in her house, then he'd come.

Shots fired at the barn.

Intruder in my house.

* * *

Carli turned the doorknob and crept to the top of the stairs. Her phone vibrated. *Now Zain responds.*

Something clanged in the kitchen.

Carli tucked her cell into her pocket. No time to answer him. She had to face this person once and for all. Another buzz.

She ignored it, pressed her body against the wall and tiptoed down, weapon raised.

Please help me, God.

One of the drawers opened. What would an intruder be looking for in her kitchen drawers? A knife?

Carli crept to the bottom of the stairs, gun ready to fire. Adrenaline rushed through her, fueling her extremities for a fight.

One, two—

"Eli, hand me that milk. I need to get it into the fridge," Marta said, her voice sounding sweeter by the second.

Carli peeked around the corner. Eli wrapped his arms around the carton, his face strained as he walked toward Marta. Carli leaned back against the wall, out of sight, and let relief wash through her. No intruder. She'd never been happier to see her loved ones at home.

She tucked the gun into the back of her jeans, inhaled a smile to her face and stepped into view.

"You're back."

"Goodness, girl. You scared me. I thought you were gone," Marta said, a hand on her chest as she glanced up from one of the bottom cupboards.

"Sorry. I parked the truck under the shed and have been upstairs."

A siren grew closer. Carli glanced out the window. Two officers pulled into her drive and stepped from the car.

"What are officers doing here?" Marta asked.

"I'll go out and talk with them."

Carli stepped onto the back porch and closed the door behind her. "So glad you're here."

"Dispatch said there was a shooting."

"Yeah. At the barn. I was able to come back to the house and hide, but haven't seen the intruder since."

"Did you get a look at the suspect?"

"Not his face. He was muscular, dark headed. Maybe six foot or a little more."

The younger cop wrote down everything she said, while the senior officer spoke. "Good. We'll check out the barn and premises. Write up a report."

"Thank you."

He pressed the button on his radio. "Dispatch. Deputy Gaines here, 416Zebra. We need backup."

A woman's voice crackled through his speaker. "Copy, 416Zebra. Sergeant Wescott will be there in five."

"Copy." Deputy Gaines released the radio switch. "Mind if we wait here until Sergeant Wescott arrives."

"Not at all."

Within a few minutes, Zain's SUV pulled into their driveway, blue lights flashing. Now she could really relax.

Eli ran out the door and hugged her legs. "I got to ride in the rocking police car at the grocery store. Do you think Zain would take me for a ride in his real police car?"

Carli squatted to his level. "Maybe later. We could certainly ask. But you know that his car doesn't rock back and forth like the one at the grocery store."

The corners of his lips turned down. "So, it's not as much fun?"

Zain's footsteps thudded onto the side porch and Carli glanced up at him. He joined the other two officers. "Dispatch said there was a shooting. Where's the intruder?"

"According to Ms. Moore, someone shot at her when she was in the old barn."

Zain faced her. "Are you okay? What happened?"

She filled him in on the scary details.

"You think he was the same guy at the bridge the other night?" Zain asked.

"Yeah. I do."

He turned back to Deputy Gaines and his

younger partner. "Go ahead and check out the barn. This guy tends to leave after the initial confrontation. If he heard the sirens, he's long gone, but see if you can find the shells and any other clues that might help with an identification. I'll stay here with the family. Make sure he doesn't come to the house if he is still on the property."

Eli waved his little hand into the air. "Come on in, Sergeant. You don't have to stand out on the porch."

Zain stepped inside and held out his hand for a low high five. "Thanks, my man. I wouldn't want you getting cold."

Eli slapped his hand and then ran back into the living area to finish his building-block creation. Zain leaned close to Carli's ear. "Are you okay?"

Carli moved to his side and placed a hand on his arm. "Excuse us for a minute, Marta. I need to chat with Zain. We'll be back in a little bit."

"Well, I'll have supper ready in an hour. Will you be staying for dinner or going back to work Sergeant Wescott?" Marta asked.

"Staying. If it's okay with Carli."

After their last argument, she understood his hesitation. They had a lot to discuss and she wanted to show him the barn after the other officers made sure it was safe. "That's fine. We've all gotta eat."

"Thank you, Marta. I accept."

Carli took his hand and led Zain to the sunroom where he'd been sleeping, then closed the door behind them when his radio clicked.

"We've checked out the old barn. All's clear. Headed back to the station to write it up," the senior deputy said.

Zain kept his gaze on her, while he answered. "Copy that. Thanks, man."

The radio went silent. Zain leaned against the glass wall opposite her and folded his arms across his chest. "You want to tell me why you went to the barn by yourself?"

"I went to look around. I got to thinking about Sadie being in there the night she was killed and wanted to see if there was anything to support our new theory. When I arrived and started poking around, someone was there. They shot at me then followed me through the stalls."

"Did you get a good look at the guy?"

"Not really. Mostly his back. But he's about six foot one, one hundred and eighty pounds, with dark hair."

"That narrows it down to about half of the town."

Carli reached into her pocket and pulled out the chain she'd discovered in the stall. "I found this."

Zain stepped forward and took the chain in his hand.

"What is it?"

"The chain from one of Sadie's necklaces. It puts her in the barn."

"How do you know this is hers?"

Carli lifted the chain from around her neck. "Because the chains are identical and she was wearing a shorter version that night. I think this is hers."

"Probably a million chains out there like that one."

Carli pointed to the delicate braided design. "I don't think so. Your sister had all her jewelry custom made. Even down to the chain. See how it almost looks like three tiny strands braided together and then twisted? She designed that with the local jeweler. This necklace had a heart on it and was about the length of a choker. But the one she gave me fell underneath her clothing, much longer."

"Hidden from view."

"Exactly."

Zain inspected the necklace closer. "If whoever took her wanted the necklace, then the shorter version wasn't the correct piece. Therefore, they discarded the chain in the old barn."

"Exactly."

"Why would they need her necklace?"

Carli lifted the locket. "Because of this."

She unfastened the necklace and fiddled the

wings of the butterfly into the shape she'd discovered before.

"The thing turns into some type of key. Figured it out today. That's why I think they've been following me or breaking into my room. No necklace was found with her remains and they've been trying to find it."

"It's definitely a key." Zain rubbed the back of his neck with his hand and exhaled a breath.

"Yeah, but to what?"

He took the object and flipped it over. Nothing displayed on the back. He opened the locket and removed the photo of her and Sadie from inside. Underneath was an inscription. "Property of the USPS."

"A post office key?" Carli asked. "But that doesn't make sense. She's been gone for over two years. Wouldn't her box be expired by now?"

"I kept paying for it."

"Why?"

"After she disappeared, I didn't have the heart to let it go. Thought maybe she'd reach out one day."

Carli took the key from him and tapped the pointed end with her fingernail. "That makes sense. I guess I just don't understand why she would camouflage this key as a locket. Why not carry a normal one like everybody else?"

"Because that's where she was stashing the drugs."

TEN

Carli stared at the green landscape passing by the open side of the covered all-terrain vehicle. Zain shared all the information he'd discovered about his sister. The drugs, her DNA at the scene, the video footage showing Sadie at the drug bust, everything. Carli's whole body refused to accept the reality that Sadie was a criminal mastermind wanted at one time by the DEA.

Not Sadie. Everyone in town loved her, thought she was the sweetest person for her dedication to her mother during her cancer treatments. She'd made the dean's list and was top of her nursing class. Never did Carli think her best friend organized and ran the local drug ring. Sure, her job gave her access to narcotics and her mother's cancer gave her motive because she needed money, but Sadie would never resort to such a low.

Thunder boomed and a bolt of lightning flared across the sky snapping Carli back to reality. Suddenly, she regretted leaving the safety of the sun porch and Marta's chicken potpie with the storm looming ahead.

"Dale told you this?"

"Yeah. Said Sadie created fake charts of deceased patients and prescribed drugs with prescription pads she stole from Dr. Frye."

Carli stared ahead, still trying to absorb the news. "That's absurd. I know Sadie would've done almost anything to help your mother, but that's illegal. Sadie would never steal from a doctor."

The look on Zain's face didn't display Carli's confidence. Seemed like he always thought the worst. Maybe that was the downside of being a cop.

He dodged another pothole in the gravel road.

"When Mom was diagnosed with cancer, we didn't have the money to pay for her treatments. Sadie said she worked extra shifts with Dr. Frye, who supposedly provided a loan for her to get Mom the medical help she needed. I thought that's how she paid for everything. Now, I'm not sure."

Carli clung to the side rail of the covered utility vehicle. If Zain ran through any more divots, she'd bounce right into his lap. At least the old barn wasn't much farther away.

His hand clung to the steering wheel in an effort to control the vehicle as a rumble of thunder rolled around them. Humid air curled his naturally wavy hair. His good looks still drew her to him. But looks weren't everything.

Another bounce popped her in the seat.

Zain glanced in her direction. "Sorry. I'm trying to hurry before this storm hits."

"Looks pretty dark near the barn. I'm not sure we'll make it before the storm. When you get there, pull inside the main aisle," she said, trying to force her mind to think about something other than the man beside her.

Raindrops the size of grapes splashed against the plastic windshield, growing into a wall of water, soaking the side of the cart. Carli scooted closer to Zain. He moved toward her as well. The sudden downpour drenched both their seats. She wrapped her fingers around his arm and tried not to focus on the nearness of him.

Zain glanced down at her hand, loosened his grip on the wheel and sent them into another divot. They bounced high. "Sorry." He recovered control of the vehicle. "Almost there."

She nodded. Nice to know she still flustered him a bit too.

They rounded the bend. The new red barn rose in height next to the older structure where Carli found Sadie's necklace.

Several of Tyler's Arabian horses huddled together underneath a group of trees. Each boom of thunder pushed the animals closer together. All except Cocoa. He darted around trying to find a way to enter into their normal shelter.

Carli leaned forward and pointed in the horses' direction. "Someone shut the main doors to the barn and the horses can't get into their stalls. They hate storms."

Carli didn't wait for Zain to park, but hopped from the ATV when it slowed. Rain pelted her body and soaked her clothes, but she didn't care. Her animals were in danger and needed her. If only she could get the door open, then direct them inside. She rushed forward, grabbed the handle and pulled.

Nothing budged.

Masculine arms enveloped her from behind and Zain placed his hands on the handle next to hers. His toned physique pressed against her back. "Let's do this on three."

He counted, his breath hot on her cheek. "One, two, three."

Carli leaned back against his chest. His strength combined with hers moved the heavy door, and it opened. All the horses shot into their new, dry spaces. Carli followed, closing their stall doors and rubbing their noses with whispered words of comfort.

Zain railed the main door closed and leaned against one of the walls, his gaze heavy on her.

She glanced in his direction. "What? They like it when I talk to them. Calms them down."

A grin tugged at the corners of his lips. "Don't mind me. I think it's sweet."

"Sweet? Ha… If only you knew the real me."

His expression changed and he grew serious. "I do know the real you, Carli." He took a step closer and leaned his broad shoulders against the stall door. "And I'm sorry."

Carli averted her gaze to the white stripe down Cocoa's nose. The air grew thick and became difficult for her to breathe.

He spoke the words she'd longed to hear for years. His presence only inches from her clouded her judgment. The walls of protection around her heart crumbled. If she dove into this conversation now, she'd never be able to turn her heart from him. Best to sidestep and hope he followed her lead.

"For what? Getting me drenched in a thunderstorm?"

He ran a hand through the wet curls atop his head and focused his eyes, the color of sea glass, on her. "You know I'm not talking about the weather. I'm sorry for accusing your brother."

Her hand stopped midstroke. She gripped the metal handle to steady herself. Cocoa whinnied a complaint. Tyler had always been a difficult subject between them. Zain's apology for all the torment he had caused was a bit late, but this was the first time she'd heard him admit his part in this whole ordeal and his words stirred mercy within her.

"Thank you. I've waited a long time to hear those words."

"I guess you have." He leaned his back against the stall door and looked up at the ceiling. "All this time, I've been focused on Tyler when Sadie was the one leading a double life. And I let her. I chose to ignore any odd behavior she displayed. Dismissed the amounts of money she paid for Mom's treatment. Never once would I have dreamed she was involved in something like this."

A bolt of lightning flashed through the windows, highlighting the tears in his eyes. Years of pain between them, both because they loved their siblings. She wanted to get past the distance, the space that kept them apart. She placed a hand on his shoulder, his shirt wet, clinging to the muscles underneath.

"I didn't make things any easier."

"No, but you did what you should've done. You stuck by your brother who you knew was innocent. Never once did you waver in your support for him. Not even when the whole town turned against the two of you and called you names, egged your house or sent you death threats.

You're strong, Carli. I don't know how you tolerated my accusations and the town's tirade against your family."

There was only one way she survived. "God helped me. Still does. Every day. He used all of the difficulties to draw me closer to Him, then took away my fear and gave me a steady peace. I know that sounds weird, but it's true."

Zain's full lips curved into that knee-weakening smile she knew too well. One of her favorite things about him. "Guess I need to spend a bit more time with God. Maybe He'd give me the wisdom I need when it comes to my sister."

Rain hammered the tin roof, echoing the pounding of her heart. She fought the urge to kiss him, to erase the years of loss and sadness with the touch of his lips. Forgiveness flowed between them, but the memories of hurt words and betrayal didn't fade as quickly. Her healed heart needed to return to Atlanta, back to her normal life where conflicting feelings and constant reminders were not part of her daily routine. Truth was, she didn't trust giving her heart to him again. Not yet. Moments like this caved in to decisions she had tried to protect against.

Carli needed a distraction. "The necklace. I need to show you where I found it."

Disappointment permeated his expression. "Right. Where do we start?"

"In the other barn. The old one."

Carli pointed to the main door. "Sounds like it's stopped raining. We'll have to cut across the field. I found the chain in the first stall. It's filled with equipment, but I think there's enough room for me to show you."

"After you."

Carli reached for the handle on the barn door and pulled. She stumbled backward when it didn't budge. "That's twice today. This thing usually slides like butter."

Zain moved to her side and bumped her elbow with his. "Guess I'm going to have to help again?"

Carli backed away to give him some room. The last thing she needed was his arms wrapped around her again, stirring up mixed feelings she wasn't ready to acknowledge. "It's stuck but feel free to give it your best yank."

Something changed between them with Zain's apology. The look of torment on his face for the choices Sadie made melted her resolve. She'd placed walls there for a reason. To never let him hurt her again. *Turn away, Carli. Don't watch him.*

She meandered over to Cocoa and petted his nose. Clearly, she and Zain still had feelings for each other, but they'd been there. Done that. Didn't work.

Zain tugged on the door with a few more forceful jerks. "The slide must've latched and jammed when I closed the exit. No worries. I'll text Nate and tell him to swing by. He wanted to see any new evidence found anyway. I'm sure he will want to get a look at the necklace."

"I could call Marta…although she doesn't like to drive through the field after a storm."

Zain held up his hand, lifted his chin and scanned the area around them. "Do you smell smoke?"

Now that he mentioned it, she wasn't sure how she didn't notice the scent before. "Yeah. And it's getting stronger."

Carli twirled in the middle of the new barn looking for any trace of a fire. Wisps of gray floated through the cracks in the walls at the opposite end.

"There. The wall's on fire."

Zain grabbed a blanket and wet it in the horse trough. He rushed toward the crack near the floor and shoved the wet material against it. "And we're locked inside."

Carli pulled out her phone, but her battery was dead. She shoved it back into her pocket. "Try the stall doors," Carli said, and darted for the side.

They tried every exit, but all of them were jammed.

Zain sniffed his fingers. "Smells like gasoline."

Additional smoke poured inside. The air grew thick, difficult to breathe. Heat permeated through the walls.

Zain opened all the interior stall doors. The horses scampered into the main aisle. Carli helped. One less thing they'd have to do once they found a way out of the growing inferno.

Zain pointed to the second-story hayloft. "Come on. There's only one way out."

Carli's eyes widened and she pulled against his hand. "We'll have to jump."

"It's the only way out. We've got to move. Once we get down, then we can unjam the main door and release the animals to the pasture."

She hated heights, but loathed fire more, and she loved her animals.

Cocoa darted around the other horses, eyes frantic. Carli had to help them. She grabbed the ladder rungs nailed to the barn post. Heat and smoke thickened with increased heights. They didn't have much time. More horses darted around below, following Cocoa's lead, and circled the barn for an escape.

Carli crawled over hay bales. Orange flames licked up the back wall. They loved dry straw. Fuel for the fire's growing appetite. Black smoke swirled around her. Her vision burned.

Zain pressed past her, unfastened the lock and pushed the hatch open. He held out his hand for Carli's. She inched her way to the side, a faintness spreading through her legs.

Zain gripped her hand tighter. "We're about twenty feet up. Only two stories. You can do this, but you're going to have to jump with me. When you land, roll to prevent injury."

Black clouds rolled in the distance. She squeezed her eyes closed. "I'm scared, Zain."

"I know, but this is the only way."

With one last look, they leapt.

Air whipped around Zain, and Carli's hand slipped from his. The jump was higher than he thought. Green grass came quick and he rolled into a soft landing. Not the easiest of falls, but he'd had worse during basic law enforcement training. A thud hit the ground behind him and Zain pressed to his feet. Carli lay sprawled out behind him. She wasn't moving.

"Carli!"

Zain rushed to her side. Blood oozed from a gash in the side of her head, a hidden rock the cause. He pressed his fingers to her neck. Pulse still there.

"Carli. Are you okay?" She didn't respond.
Dear God, let her wake up.

He pressed a hand over the cut and wished

he'd found another way out. An axe to a wall or something other than making her jump.

He reached for his cell to call 911 when her eyes fluttered open. He'd never been happier to hear her groan.

"Don't move. You might have a head or neck injury. I'll get the truck and take you to the hospital."

Firm fingers grasped his arm and her gaze locked with his. "The horses. Let them out."

"What about you?"

"I'm fine. It's just a little bump, but the horses will die if we don't get them out."

Zain helped her sit up, then rushed back to the barn. He shoved against the sliding door, but nothing moved. He pressed his shoulder against the side. Still didn't budge. He inspected the tract. A small board was lodged into the tray. Someone had locked them inside.

He dug out the slat and slid the door open. Black and brown horses skirted around him, panicked from all the smoke inside. The stampede charged into fresh pasture.

He glanced over at Carli, who was sitting up, wide-eyed. "Where's Cocoa?"

Zain scanned the area again. Cocoa was not with the team.

Carli pushed to her feet, stumbling toward the burning barn. He rushed to her side. "You can't go in there. The whole place is about to be engulfed."

She quickened her stride. "I'm not leaving him."

Carli stumbled again, bumping into his shoulder. Zain steadied her. "You don't need to be walking. You might have a head injury."

"I've got to save him. I'm his only hope."

He handed her his cell phone. "I'll go find him. You stay here and call 911."

Zain grabbed another blanket hanging near the first stall. He dunked the material into a trough filled with water, then covered himself and entered the smoky haze. Flames danced up opposite walls and into the rafters. Cocoa's stall was empty. He spun around, scanning the area. A dark shadow moved deeper in the building.

Cocoa stood by the hayloft ladder.

The last place he'd seen Carli.

Zain rushed to his side and pressed against him. "Yah."

The black Arabian horse reared up on his hind legs. Zain backed up. His front legs came down with a thud and he circled in front of him. Skittish. Panicked. He threw the blanket onto the horse's back and slapped his backside. "Go on, get!"

He skirted around him again, releasing high-pitched screams. Carli moved into the barn, her face highlighted by the increasing flames. She stood inside the entrance. "Come on, Cocoa."

The horse darted straight for her, then dashed into the open air.

The fire roared behind Zain, cracking a rafter. Heat bore down on his skin. He had to get out of there. He moved toward the front. A fiery beam fell to the floor in front of him. His only exit blocked.

"Zain!" Carli's yell was barely audible above the whoosh of flames.

Fire circled on all sides. Smoke enveloped the oxygen he needed to breathe and burned his eyes. He had to find another way out.

Cocoa's stall, to the left. He'd have to break through the door, locked by their attacker. He scanned the hazy area around him. A darkened corner housed equipment. He stumbled over. A wooden handle stuck up from behind a front bucket meant for a large tractor. He grabbed the tool and lifted. A sledgehammer.

Zain moved back to the stall. He lifted the heavy tool and let it drop with force. Each swing struck solid wood, increasing the pounding in his head. His energy faded. Oxygen escaped him, and carbon monoxide stole his life-giving breaths. Muscles ached from the effort, but the door remained intact. The room began to spin and an orange blaze increased around him, blurring his vision. Sirens blared nearby. *Hurry.*

Zain lowered the hammer and dropped to the floor. Better air there. Buy more time. Darkness invaded his vision.

Carli. He had to survive for her.

But the heat was unbearable and toxins filled his lungs. A strong crack echoed behind him. He tried to force his eyes open to see. They wouldn't move.

Another crack. A rush of cool air whipped over him. He drank in the fresh oxygen. Voices. Male. Strong arms hooked underneath his shoulders and lifted his body. Someone pulled Zain to safety, the sledgehammer still in his grasp.

He was lifted, placed on a soft mattress. Pain spread through his chest when he inhaled and moved into his left arm. Zain clutched his chest.

"He needs oxygen."

A paramedic placed a mask over his nose and mouth. "We need to get moving. Skin is pale and clammy. Lips, cyanotic. Get those EKG leads on him. Make sure he's not going into cardiac arrest."

Nate stood beside him, the lines in his friend's forehead deepened. "Zain, can you talk?"

He wanted to, but when he tried nothing but wheezes and coughs emerged. "Take him. I'll stay with Carli and her brother. I need to get their statements and make sure she gets checked out too."

Her brother?

Zain scanned the gathered crowd as the orange blaze lit the night sky. Flames soared into the air above the roofline. The new barn destroyed. At least he saved Carli and her horses. He scanned every face for hers.

Off to the side, she sat on a stretcher, the same oxygen mask over her nose. She stared at him with tear-filled eyes. And there, next to her, Carli's brother stood.

Tyler was home.

Zain tried to sit up, to motion them over, but everyone pushed him back into place and lifted the stretcher into the ambulance.

He had to talk to Tyler. Get his questions answered.

Present all the evidence to his lieutenant, so Tyler's name could be cleared and Sadie's real killer could be brought to justice.

Zain pulled at the oxygen mask and two strong hands secured his arms at his side.

A pierce underneath the skin secured the IV, and injected meds forced the trauma of the night to fade into oblivion.

ELEVEN

Daylight broke through the hospital window, waking Carli from her restless sleep on the hard vinyl couch placed in the room for relatives. She wasn't family, but Ms. Wescott stayed most of the night and had to leave. Zain's mother needed to rest in her own bed.

Marta took the woman home and Carli promised she wouldn't leave Zain's side until his mother returned the next morning.

Carli reached for the Tylenol bottle in her bag and dropped two pills into her palm. Her head still pounded from her own injuries. Nothing serious except for the goose egg–sized knot taking up residence on her forehead. Could've been much worse.

At least one good thing came with last night's disaster. Tyler was home. They hadn't had much time to talk yet, but Eli was happy to see his father. She'd given him a welcome-home hug and come straight to the hospital.

Zain was her most important priority at the moment. He'd suffered second-degree burns on his right leg after the flames ignited his jeans. The doctor said his injuries were not life-threatening and should heal in a couple of weeks.

Carli's phone vibrated, tearing her thoughts away from the nightmarish memories. A good distraction.

"Hello?"

"Finally. About time I got ahold of you. I called like three times last week. Why didn't you return my phone calls?"

Celeste, her Atlanta colleague, often liked to call and discuss hours of work-related topics, but with all the drama in her life lately, the last thing she wanted was more issues on her plate. "I've been a little busy with my nephew and the ranch."

Her gaze stayed on Zain, the oxygen cannula in his nose, intravenous lines running in all directions and the incessant beep of monitors recording his vital signs. They'd given him sedatives last night to help him rest and let his lungs recover, but she'd love to see his blue eyes open.

"You've got to get back to Atlanta. Sheila has decided you've been gone too much and are shirking your duties. She's given two of your top clients away to a new girl she hired."

Sheila was Carli's manager and a self-professed workaholic. She often called after work hours to discuss clients and punished her employees with difficult accounts when they didn't pick up.

"I can't come back right now. Zain and I were in a fire last night."

"What? Are you okay?"

"Yeah. I'm fine. Just bruised up. They kept Zain overnight for observation, but they say he's doing better."

Carli stood and gazed out the window. She'd stay by his side as long as it took for him to heal. The man saved her life and seeing him almost die to save her horse was enough to wake up her frozen heart. She loved him. Time for them to work through a few things.

"You want me to talk to her? Tell her what happened?"

"No. I'll call her later. Probably need to discuss a few logistics anyway."

"Okay, friend. I'll be honest. I can't wait till you get back. I've missed you around here. Talk to you later."

Carli ended the call and took in the view of the mountains. The layers of rock rising up on the horizon comforted her soul. This was home and she wanted to stay. For Zain.

He was still sleeping. She wished her night had been as calm. Instead, her body ached. Perhaps some coffee would help wake her up. She made her way down to the small kitchen set aside for family use, when Dr. Candyce Frye rounded the corner.

"Hi, Carli. I heard about Zain. How's he doing?"

"They sedated him. Gave him medicine to help him sleep. He was pretty restless last night."

"I can imagine." Dr. Frye's gaze drifted to Carli's forehead. "How are you doing? Looks like you took a few blows also. Do you need me to write another prescription for pain medication? I'm sure you're out by now after the injury to your leg."

"No, thanks. I'm good, shaken up a bit, but physically fine. Zain and I had to jump from the hayloft to escape the fire. I hit my head on a rock."

"That sounds dreadful. I'm sorry you're going through all of this. Maybe they'll catch the arsonist who did this to you."

Carli took note of her statement. "How'd you know it was arson?"

Candyce smiled at a nurse passing by and glanced back to Carli. "It's a small town. Word travels fast at Heather's."

Dr. Frye held up her coffee cup with the shop's logo on the side.

"Seems like the whole town goes there every

morning." Carli pointed toward the coffeepot inside the family lounge. "I was headed to get a cup of joe myself. I'm sure it's not as good as Heather's though."

"She does make a mean mug. I like to go and visit most of my patients who happen to stop by. I can check on them there, plus listen to the gossip and find out if anyone else needs my services."

"Well, it was nice talking to you."

"You too." Candyce started to pass by her, then stopped. "I know you've been here for several weeks. Don't you have to get back to Atlanta soon?"

The question seemed out of the blue. Maybe the good doctor wanted her away from Zain, then she could sink her well-manicured claws into him. There was no doubt in Carli's mind that Candyce liked him.

"With the fire and everything, I'm planning to stay a bit longer, maybe take some family leave. I want to help Tyler get the barn rebuilt."

The woman forced a smile to her face. Didn't quite make it all the way to her eyes. "Great. Well, I guess I'll be seeing you."

Pain shot from Zain's toes all the way into his hip. He tried to grab for his leg, but something held him down, or someone. Was he still strapped to the stretcher?

He opened his eyes wide. Bright light assaulted his vision. Loud beeps intensified with the ache in his head. Oxygen blared through a tube in his nose.

Dale was there with a nurse. Holding down his arms.

"Zain, calm down, buddy. She's trying to give you some pain meds. Stop fighting."

The nurse attached another bag and pressed a few buttons on the pump. The pain began to fade. Dale's hand loosened on his arm, but Zain grasped the man's wrist.

"Carli?"

Dale patted his hand. "She's fine. A few bumps and bruises, but absolutely fine. In fact, she's still here. I saw her headed into the family lounge for coffee."

She was safe. Uninjured. That's all that mattered.

Images of last night replayed in Zain's mind. Flames covered his leg right before the paramedics pulled him to safety. A few more minutes and he might've been reunited with Sadie, but here he was in a hospital bed. "And Tyler?"

Dale took a seat next to his bed. "We can talk about that in a few days, when you're feeling better."

"He's innocent."

His friend leaned forward and clasped his hands together. "Not so sure about that."

Zain tried to sit up and focus, but the pain medications were definitely taking their toll. "I've got more—"

Dale's strong hand fell to his shoulder. "Just rest and listen. The sledgehammer you pulled from the barn last night had some blood residue on it. At first, we thought it was yours, but that didn't seem quite right. Then we ran it through the lab in Asheville. One of my DEA buddies owed me a favor and got the results back to me this morning."

Zain kept his focus. "And?"

"The sledgehammer was the weapon used to kill Sadie. Tyler's fingerprints are all over it. We got him, man. This is the smoking gun that's going to put Tyler Moore away for life."

Disappointment twisted inside his chest with the news. Carli would be devastated and likely to not believe the condemning evidence. Zain tried to think of an alternative angle, like he knew Carli would do. "Of course his fingerprints would be on the hammer because he uses it on the ranch. I'm not sure that's a smoking gun."

Darkness flashed through Dale's eyes and his face tightened. "And do you think it was a co-incidence that the barn caught on fire with you inside the same night Tyler returned home?"

"We don't know he was the one to set the barn on fire. Why would he burn his own building down? Doesn't make any sense."

Dale stood up and paced the floor. "What's with you? One minute you're adamant this guy killed Sadie and then the next you're acting all wishy-washy. Is this about Carli?"

He couldn't tell him yes even though the answer was partly true. Carli raised some good points about the innocence of her brother. "Of course not. Last time we questioned Tyler we didn't have enough evidence to hold him. I want to make sure we have the right guy this time."

"What more evidence do you need, Zain? We found Sadie's body on his property, he was the last one to see and call her, and now we have the murder weapon with his prints retrieved from his barn. All the pieces are right in front of you. Forget what Carli thinks and do your job."

All the facts did point to Tyler, but they didn't fit together in his gut. Carli helped him to see the cracks in the case against her brother.

"Why would Tyler break into his own home and ransack Carli's bedroom? He would never harm Carli. Also, the texts Carli received threatened Eli, Tyler's son. No father would do something like that."

His friend paced to the window and looked out. "I don't know. My old man was mean and as for the break-in, the police report didn't tie it to Sadie's case. Said it was a separate incident. Before the night is over, Tyler Moore will be behind bars. Mark my words. One more bad guy off the streets."

Zain pressed the button to raise the head of his bed. "Don't do this, Dale. I think the man's innocent."

"Those meds really are clouding your judgment on this one." He stepped back to the bed and placed a hand on Zain's shoulder. "You just rest and get better. Let me and Nate handle this. If anyone deserves justice, Sadie does."

"Don't do this yet. I'm telling you—"

"I'll come back by tomorrow."

Dale left and Zain closed his eyes. The pounding in his head might go away if he'd relax. But how could he relax when Tyler was about to be arrested. He'd failed again.

Soft footsteps entered the room with the scent of vanilla. *Carli.*

He opened his eyes and drank in her beauty. Even the purpled bruise on her head did little to mask the petite features of her pretty face. Sunlight brushed through the window and bathed her red hair with gold. He reached for her hand. Her green eyes brightened with a smile. "You're awake. I was worried."

She moved to the edge of the bed and took a seat.

Zain didn't want her to return to Atlanta, but going back to the city was the only thing that would keep her safe. He'd never forgive himself if something happened to her.

She tied a get-well balloon to the chair. "I've got some good news. Tyler's home and I've decided to stay at the ranch. I'm going to call my Atlanta firm and resign. I never really liked that job anyway. I've got so many ideas for running the ranch. We can do weddings, corporate events and parties, along with all the horse trading Tyler does. I think we could make something great together. Bring it back to what Mom and Dad would've wanted if they were here. Plus, I can help with your recov—"

"Don't." The pain in his chest was no longer triggered by smoke inhalation.

She sat a bit straighter at his response. "Don't what?"

When she found out about Tyler, she'd never look at him the same.

She needed to go back to Atlanta. Get away from this town. Her life would be in even more danger once the news of Tyler's arrest came out.

"I've got some news too. Tyler's going to be arrested. The sledgehammer I used last night in the fire was tested and had Sadie's blood on it along with Tyler's fingerprints."

Carli lowered herself into the visitor chair. "No, that can't be."

"Dale had a friend at one of his labs run the test and the results came back positive. He came by and told me a few minutes ago. The decision's been made and it's out of my hands."

"And you just let him walk out of here with no argument. Why didn't you tell him about the necklace, the threatening texts, the bullet casings we—"

"I tried—"

She stood, her fists clenched by her side. "You didn't try hard enough."

Carli grabbed her leather bag and rounded the bed. "I've got to go stop them."

He sat up and touched her arm. "You can't stop them, Carli. It's too late. I hope you called your lawyer. Tyler's going to need him now more than ever."

No words came from her rose-painted lips. Only a cold dark look passed to him before she turned away and stormed from the room.

TWELVE

Carli ran across the front porch and into the house. "Tyler! We've got to go. Hurry! Tyler?"

His boots clamored across the kitchen floor and into the great room where Carli stood. "What's going on?"

She crossed to him and grabbed his arm, pulling him toward his bedroom. "Where's Eli and Marta?"

"They went to pick strawberries and then had some errands to run. I don't think the guard was too happy about spending his day in the field. Why?"

"We've got to get out of here. Where's your suitcase? I'll pack your things while you get Eli's bag ready."

Tyler placed his hands on Carli's shoulders. "Sis—stop for a minute and tell me why we have to leave."

His face grew blurry from the tears burning

her eyes. "They're going to arrest you for Sadie's murder and we need to get you out of here."

Tyler leaned against the back of the couch.

Carli grabbed his hands and pulled. "We've got very little time."

"I'm not running, Carli."

Every muscle fiber inside her tensed. "But you're innocent. You didn't kill Sadie and you can't let them pin this on you. We've got to leave this crazy town. They'll forget all about us in a few months."

"God doesn't want us to run from our fears, sis. He wants us to stand strong and fight."

Carli sobbed into his arms. "Then my decision is made. I'm staying at the ranch. I'll run the place, take care of Eli and fight for your freedom with you. Marta and I will be able to handle everything here."

Tyler dropped his arms and paced to the window. "There's only one problem. I wanted to talk to you about it tonight over dinner." He turned to face her. "I want to sell the ranch."

His words punched the air from her lungs. What was it with the men in her life lately? Did they have some conspiracy to destroy every good thing she loved?

"What are you talking about? Running the ranch has been your dream since Mom and Dad died. They left this place to us. We can't sell it."

"That's where you're wrong. I never wanted to run the ranch. My dream was to finish law school. The ranch was never my dream. Maybe you don't remember, but I dropped out after the accident happened and came home. I got married while in law school and had Eli, but when Ava was killed in the accident with Mom and Dad, I started to think about life differently. The only reason I took over the ranch was for you. You needed to finish college. I had to step up and be the man of the house and provide for my little sister and son."

Carli sank to the couch. "We can't sell now. Not until we find Sadie's real killer."

"I know. We're going to have to call that lawyer of yours to beat this charge once and for all. Then we can both chase our dreams."

All his plans bounced off her like a Ping-Pong ball. "Sounds like you've got it all figured out."

Tyler took a scat beside her on the couch. "There's nothing left in this town for us, sis. Everyone hates us and kids can be cruel when they get into grade school. I don't want Eli to be bullied like us. I can't put him through that kind of torment. That was the reason for the business trip. I met with several interested buyers and we have an offer. A good one. It will pay for more than any lawyer fees."

"I'm not ready for us to sell this place. We

can use the business trust that Mom and Dad set aside to pay for the attorney, plus I have money in savings we can use to fight this."

"I can't let you use your savings or quit your job in Atlanta. I'm not going to have you give up everything to keep me out of jail."

How did she tell her brother she really didn't want to return to Atlanta? Her whole plan had been to stay.

"I'll take care of it. You've been at this for a long time now. Let me oversee a few things. I think Joe, our main ranch hand, would do a good job with the day-to-day, don't you?"

Tyler nodded. "He'd be great. Practically runs the place anyway."

Dust stirred outside the living room windows as two cop cars pulled into the drive. Carli took his hand in hers. "I'll call the lawyer now and we'll get you out on bail."

Tyler forced a sad smile. "I hope so. Will you tell Eli I love him and give him a kiss for me? Tell him I'll be back soon."

"Of course."

She hated this. He should be here giving Eli kisses and tucking him in at night. Footsteps thumped on the porch. Tyler squeezed her fingers.

"Would you think me weak if I told you I was scared?"

She gripped his hands tighter. "I'm scared too. But God will get us through this."

"He always has."

"He always will."

Two loud knocks caused her to flinch. Tyler released her hands and walked to the door.

Dale and Nate stood on the other side. No more than an inch of glass keeping them away from her brother.

Tyler invited the officers inside. "What can I do for you?"

Carli rose and joined her brother. Strength in numbers.

Dale handed him a folded piece of paper. "We've got an arrest warrant for you, Tyler."

Carli took a step forward and raised her chin. She glanced around Dale and eyed Nate, who kept his gaze to the floor. "Are y'all really going to go through all this again when our lawyer destroyed your case the first time around?"

Dale stepped forward with a smirk on his face. "You betcha. There's been new evidence."

Carli didn't back away. "What new evidence?"

Zain had already shared with her about the murder weapon, but she didn't want them to know he'd told her.

"We found the weapon that murdered Sadie Wescott. A sledgehammer in Tyler's new barn with her blood on it and his fingerprints."

Two deputies pushed past her, moved through the door and disappeared down the hallway. "Where are they going?"

"To do a search. That's part of our warrant too."

Dale reached for his cuffs and slapped them on Tyler's wrist before she could muster up an objection.

"Tyler Moore, you're under arrest for the murder of Sadie Wescott."

Her eyes locked with Tyler's as Dale dragged him out the door, continuing to state his rights.

Her brother remained calm. "Carli, call our lawyer. I'll be fine. Don't forget what I told you to tell Eli."

She nodded at his instructions, numb to the deputies going through her brother's things and carrying out his laptop, cell phone and anything else tied to him. She kept her phone tucked away in her pocket. After all, she wasn't the suspect.

Dale ducked her brother's head into the cruiser, closed the door and headed out of the driveway.

Nate still stood on her porch, a passive bystander to this atrocity. "I'm sorry, Carli."

She pulled Nate to the side, away from the listening ears of the other deputies parading in and out of her house. "Dale seems to be the one driving this campaign against my brother. Right?"

"He's with the DEA and Sadie's death is

wrapped up with one of their cases. He's the one pulling the strings and making the decisions."

She'd lived through this once and they'd won. She'd do it again. Take on the entire town to fight for her brother. This time they'd clear his name for good.

Carli stepped within inches of Nate's face, her teeth clenched. "You head on back to your station and tell Lieutenant Black that if he thought he saw all our fight the last time they did this to my brother, then he hasn't seen anything yet. And tell Zain he needs to figure out whose side he's on, because if he gets in my way, I'll take him down too."

Nate rubbed the stubble on his chin. "You know Zain's being discharged this afternoon. He'll be back home in case you need anything."

Was Zain sending her some kind of message through Nate? She took a step back. "Good. Because he's going to need to rest up to find Sadie's real murderer."

Carli left Nate and headed inside. All the officers finally rolled out of their home around noon. Nothing left to do now but sit on the porch and cry.

Dusk turned to dark. Marta returned with Eli around supper time and fixed some soup and sandwiches, then Carli let her nephew watch one of his favorite television shows before bed. That was the least they could do for him after the devastating news about Tyler.

Carli slipped into his room and tucked the covers tight around him.

"When's Dad going to be home again?" Eli asked.

His question ripped through every sidestepping movement she'd made to keep from discussing the subject. Carli leaned forward and planted a kiss on his forehead. "Soon. And I'll be right here until he gets back. No worries, okay?"

Eli snuggled his teddy bear close. "Okay. Love you, Aunt Carli."

"Love you too, bud."

She made it to her bathroom before more sobs hit. With one turn of the sink faucet she let hot water run over a washcloth and pressed the warmth to her red, puffy face. She breathed in the steam.

How could this be happening again?

Her brother was sitting in a cold jail cell, his dreams of going to law school destroyed. The man had lost his parents, his wife and potentially his freedom. She had to convince the lawyer to take his case. The Atlanta attorney didn't hesitate the first time, but now with the mounting evidence against her brother, she wasn't as confident.

A scream pierced the quiet of the home. Carli dropped the cloth and bolted into the hallway.

"Marta?"

"He's not here!"

"What are you talking about?"

"Eli… He's not in his bed. It hasn't been more than ten minutes since you turned out his light, but he's gone."

Her friend's eyes were wide and glassy. Marta's hands shook as she motioned toward the empty bed. Carli glanced into the little boy's room, then moved down the hall.

"He probably went to the bathroom or got hungry." She fought the familiar heart palpitations building in her chest. "I'm sure he's fine."

Carli checked Eli's usual spots. He wasn't there.

Her footsteps quickened, then turned into a jog, rushing from room to room, yelling his name, upstairs and down. She searched all his favorite outside places for three hours. Eli was not on the premises.

With one last effort, Carli reentered the house. "Eli? Honey, answer me. If you're hiding, please come out. I need to know you're okay."

Carli hoped to hear his cute snicker from a secret place. Only the distant bark of a dog interrupted the silence.

Heaviness invaded every limb of Carli's body

as she climbed the stairs, back to her nephew's bedroom. Marta still stood, leaned against the door frame. With one look at Carli, the woman crumpled to the floor in sobs. "I kept praying you'd find him."

Carli entered her nephew's bedroom. A faint wisp of moonlight dusted the empty white sheets with a haunting glow. Only the imprint of his head on the pillow remained beside his favorite stuffed bear. He slept with Wigley every night. No way Eli would leave him behind if he had a choice.

She'd call Zain. Wait. Not Zain. He was the last person she wanted to see. Nate. She'd call Nate.

Carli glanced at the time on her phone. 1:00 a.m. A text message alert displayed on her screen.

I told you Eli was next.

Carli slid down the wall and sank to the floor. "They've got Eli."

Marta's wails pierced her own heart. "Dear God, please no."

The woman curled into a ball and began to rock back and forth on the floor. "Please, Father God, protect him. I beg you. Please, Father..."

Her sobs turned into groans, indiscernible to

any ear. Carli had to do something. Her fingers swiped the keyboard as she texted a reply.

What do you want? I'll give you anything. Money. Myself. Just don't hurt my nephew.

A flashing ellipse appeared and taunted her from the bottom of her screen.

We want the evidence Sadie gave you and the money. Two million. Bring it to the old airstrip at the edge of the county Friday. 6:00 p.m. No cops or the boy's dead.

"Evidence? What evidence?"

Marta stopped the rocking motion and stared at her. "What are you talking about?"

"I've got less than a day to find this evidence and take it to the old airstrip at the edge of the county, but I'm not sure what they are talking about."

Marta scooted next to Carli and glanced at her screen. "You're texting them?"

"Negotiating. I'm trying to get more information. Find out what they want, then we can get Eli back."

"And?"

"They want the evidence Sadie gave me, but she never gave me anything. Except this necklace." Carli clutched the locket in her hand. "I forgot about the key… Zain and I never made it to the post office."

They'd planned to go after they visited the barn, but then the fire broke out. The post office box was the last thing on their mind.

She pressed up from the floor, slipped on her tennis shoes and grabbed her bag. "I've got to go."

"Where are you going? It's late."

She had to go get Zain. He was the only one who could help her. Zain knew Skye Anderson, a supervisor for the local post office. She'd need him to get her inside to find whatever was in Sadie's box.

"I'm going to get Eli back."

Loud rapping on the front door woke Zain from his already fitful sleep. His leg throbbed as he tossed the sheet back and let his leg dangle over the edge of the bed for a minute. Another round of knocking ensued.

"Coming," he yelled. Nerves in his leg burned in protest to the sudden change in position. He pressed his good foot to the ground and grabbed the hospital cane to help disperse his weight when he walked.

He made it to the door and peered out the window. Carli stood with her hair tossed into a messy bun on top of her head and paced back and forth on his front porch.

Nate had passed along her message. Her words had plagued his dreams all night. He understood she felt betrayed, especially after everything that happened between them in the barn, but Dale was right. He couldn't ignore evidence and let his feelings for Carli cloud the oath he promised to uphold when he joined the sheriff's department. He had to do his job.

Zain flicked on the outside light and opened the front door.

"Carli? What are you doing here?"

Her eyes were wide. She handed him her phone and stepped inside before he could offer a proper invitation.

"They've got Eli."

"What?"

"Somehow they took him from our house tonight. They must've slipped him out."

Zain held up a hand. "Wait. Slow down. Who has Eli?"

"I don't know." She motioned toward her phone. "They sent me those messages and he's not in his room. Said to bring them the evidence Sadie left me or they will hurt him. We can't let that happen."

Carli paced the hardwood floor, her hands frantic with motion. "I've got to find him and I need you to call Skye Anderson."

Her thought process was leaps beyond his. He

had to catch up and quick if Eli had been kidnapped. "Skye Anderson? What does she have to do with this?"

Carli took two strides, lifted her chin and locked eyes with him. "For once, would you please trust me? Is that too much to ask?"

"Not at all. I'm trying to catch up with what's happening."

She backed away a step. "I need her to open the post office for me. You owe me, Zain. That's the least you can do after the trouble you've caused my family."

He handed back her phone. "I don't have a problem calling Skye. I want to know why. You need in the post office because?"

She shoved the phone into her back pocket and started to pace again. "Because of the necklace, remember. You were the one who showed me the key went to a PO box. Even you said that's where Sadie stashed the drugs. Maybe these people want their merchandise back, and I can't go empty-handed."

The key. To his sister's PO box. Now everything was coming back. The trauma had done a number on his memory. "Let me put on some better clothes and then I'll call Skye. But you're not meeting these people alone. We'll get a team together."

Carli spun toward him. "No. No cops. They

said they'd kill Eli if I brought cops. I'll go alone. I can handle myself."

"Are you crazy? If this is some drug ring, there's no way I'm letting you go alone."

She shook her head and turned back toward the door. "You'll get him killed. I'm doing this without you."

"Don't you get it, Carli? I can't live with myself if something happens to you. My sister is dead and I'm not letting you end up in the ground with her. Nate and I are trained to handle hostage situations. I'm not letting you do this alone. When we go for the exchange, they won't know we're there, but we *are* going. Either you can cooperate or find another way into the post office."

She stopped in her tracks and faced him. "Fine. But hurry, we don't have any time to waste."

Zain changed his clothes, then drove them into town. Everything was dark except for the glow of a few streetlamps on Main Street that cast circled spotlights onto the sidewalk. His SUV was the only vehicle on the road.

He found a parking spot, cut the engine and pulled out his phone. Two thirty in the morning. They had less than sixteen hours to find the evidence, figure out who was behind Eli's kidnapping and make the exchange.

"Skye texted me. Said she'd be here in about five minutes. She's running a little late."

Carli unbuckled her seat belt and stared out the passenger window. "She used to date my brother for a while after his wife died. I think she really liked him, but he couldn't move past his grief."

"How long ago was that?"

"I don't know. Maybe a year."

Right before Zain took Skye out. Nate had encouraged him to get back in the dating game after Carli left town and the woman was single.

Carli glanced toward him. "I guess she's your ex-girlfriend too?"

Had she been keeping tabs on him after she moved? Probably found out from her brother. "Not exactly. We didn't really have anything in common, but she's a nice woman."

"I always liked her. I think she would've been good with Tyler and a sweet person to help raise Eli, but I guess it wasn't meant to be. How long did the two of you date?"

"I wouldn't really call going to a restaurant and one night of bowling dating. We decided we're better off as friends."

Truth was he never got over Carli, but he kept that information to himself.

"I see." She fidgeted in her seat. "This is taking forever. Why can't people be on time?"

A smile tugged at the corners of his lips at her impatience. Her punctuality was a trait he admired. "It's almost three a.m. I'm sure she wasn't expecting to be disturbed in the middle of the night. Probably needed a few minutes to get dressed and speed over here."

Carli pointed to the street. "There she is."

Skye emerged from the alley next to the building and walked toward the post office door, keys in hand. They crossed the street and joined her.

"Well, if it isn't Carli Moore. I thought you'd be back in Atlanta by now."

A hesitant smile surfaced on Carli's face, the look of relief evident. Zain never knew if any of their old friends were going to be kind or attack. Skye was different than most. She usually formed her own opinions and didn't let gossip sway her. Too bad everyone in this world couldn't be the same way.

"I can't leave Tyler right now and we need your help. Can you let us in? My brother's son is missing."

Skye stiffened at the mention of Tyler and Eli. He'd heard the woman still hoped they'd reconcile. Be a family. Looked like Zain wasn't the only one to have a Moore wreak havoc on a heart.

The post office door clicked unlocked, but Skye kept her hand on the handle. "How is Tyler?"

Carli glanced at her. "Not good at the moment. He's been arrested and I'm hoping what we find here tonight will help clear his name.

But I haven't told him about Eli yet. The news will destroy him."

Skye pressed her thumb down on the latch. "If there's anything more I can do to help, let me know. Okay?"

Carli nodded. "Thanks."

The door swung open and Zain followed the two women inside. Metal boxes lined the walls and jutted into the center of the room, forming aisles of mailboxes similar to the stacks in a library.

Skye held out her palm toward him. "You did bring the paperwork, right? I can't let you go opening Sadie's mailbox if you don't have the power of attorney documents."

Zain handed her the previously notarized forms. After Sadie became a nurse, she made sure her entire family had all their medical and legal documents in order. He never thought he'd be the one using hers. "Here ya go."

Skye gave them a cursory glance. "Do I need to look up Sadie's PO box number or do you know it?"

"It's box eighty-two," Carli said, moving toward the aisle with matching numbers.

Zain followed. "How'd you know?"

"She wrote the number on the back of our photo. The one stuck on her dresser."

"Doesn't mean that's her box number."

"Just going with my gut here, Wescott. If only

you'd learn to trust me, then we'd all have fewer headaches."

Carli twisted the key into the lock. The box opened.

Crammed inside was a manila envelope that Zain removed and motioned for Skye.

"How'd this package get in here? I've been checking this box up until a few months ago. Nothing but junk mail. Where did this come from?"

Skye flipped the package in her hand. "Not sure. There's no return address, but someone had to pay postage to mail it. I could look the confirmation number up for you and see what information we have listed."

"Thanks."

Skye handed back the package and disappeared toward the main desk.

Zain retrieved a couple pairs of plastic gloves for them to wear, then opened the back flap.

Inside were prescription bottles. He removed them a couple at a time, reading the details on the front. Oxycodone, fentanyl and other narcotics. Was she delivering drugs like Dr. Frye said, or was Sadie dealing prescription meds on the black market to pay for his mother's cancer treatments? Only one idea made sense and he didn't want to believe his sister broke the law. Or even worse, her actions got her killed.

Carli lifted several of the bottles from his open

palm. "All the patients with names on these bottles are dead."

She held one up for him to read. "Ms. Rita Greene died a year before Sadie was killed and here is a bottle with the woman's name on it long after she was gone. Howard Bruce died ten years ago."

"You know them?"

"They used to come by the ranch a lot. Liked horses."

"Then it's true. Sadie was selling these drugs on the black market. Just like Dale said."

"Unless she discovered someone else's scheme and planned to expose them."

"What do you mean?"

Carli held up the container in her hand. "The text I got requested I bring the evidence, not the merchandise or the goods. Like whatever Sadie had given me would somehow be used against these people. What if Sadie uncovered their operation and planned to go to the cops?"

Her theory made sense and fit Sadie's character better than any other explanation. "Then that would give them motive to kill her."

"Exactly."

Skye headed back around the corner with a notepad in hand. "Looks like the package was mailed here at this facility, went to a processing plant in Greenville and then back to Sadie's box."

"Then who mailed it?"

Skye shrugged her shoulders. "We don't take down the names of the people that drop off the packages, and without any identifying name or address on the front of the envelope, that information wouldn't be in our database."

Zain twisted one of the bottles in his hand. "Do you have a date?"

"Yeah, right here."

Skye pointed to the top of her notes and Zain read the numbers. "That's the day after we found Sadie's body. I need to see any security videos you have from this day."

"Sure."

Skye led them to a small office behind the main counter. She started up their computers, typed in her username and password, then pulled up the footage with the same date and approximate time stamp.

In walked a familiar face with the manila package in hand.

"Candyce."

The good Dr. Frye handed the package to the clerk across the counter and gave him a sweet smile. Let's see how much she smiled when Zain brought her in for questioning.

THIRTEEN

Carli stood in the parking lot of the Henderson County jail at nine on Friday morning, waiting for her brother to be released on bail. The court had called early to pick him up.

While she waited, Carli tapped Zain's number. Hopefully, he had some news about Candyce.

"Well? Did you get her to confess?"

"I wish. The good doctor was appalled I called her to the station and treated her like a common criminal."

"Which she is, right?"

His sigh on the other end of the call was not encouraging. "Not exactly. Sadie gave Candyce the package two years ago and told her if anything ever happened to her then Candyce needed to mail it to the PO box address. Candyce put the package in a drawer and didn't think any more about it—"

"Until we found Sadie's body."

"Exactly. She saw the news interview I did and

then she carried out her friend's last wish. Says she didn't even know what was inside or that the address belonged to Sadie."

They had nine hours before meeting Eli's captors. Carli had hoped to have some encouraging news.

Now she had to tell Tyler the devastating news about Eli.

An alarm echoed across the black asphalt.

"Gotta go, Zain. I'll call ya later."

Carli stepped from the car and opened the passenger-side door while a guard escorted Tyler to the gate, then uncuffed him. She gave her brother a big hug and motioned to the car.

"Get in. I've got something to tell you."

"Okay." He did as instructed and faced her in the seat. "What's wrong? Today's a day for celebrating. I thought the judge was going to lock me up until the trial and I'd end up in a jail cell for weeks. We need cake or ice cream or something."

Carli stared at the forest of trees lining the pavement and gripped the steering wheel tighter. "Eli's missing."

Her brother slumped back against the passenger-side door. "What?"

"Someone took him from our home last night after the cops arrested you. People were going in and out of the house yesterday afternoon. Everything was chaotic."

The sob in her throat thickened as the events replayed in her mind. "I took Eli to his room to tuck him in at bedtime, but about fifteen minutes later he was missing."

Tears filled his eyes and he blinked, releasing their wetness to his cheeks. "Did you check his tree house? Sometimes, when he gets scared, he likes to climb up there and fish in the creek below."

"We've checked everywhere. The tree house, the barn, the cave…everywhere."

"And where were you? You were supposed to be taking care of him, protecting him."

She blamed herself too. If she'd been more alert, observant, responsible, Eli would still be here. Sadie would still be here. Bad things happened when she was around. "I tried everything I could think of to find him."

"Take me home. I need to get back and start searching for him. Did the police issue an Amber Alert?"

"I got a message from the kidnappers and if we involve the cops, then they'll hurt him. So we didn't issue any Amber Alerts."

Tyler slapped the dash with his palm. "Well, great. Get me home."

Carli stepped on the gas and kept quiet the rest of the way to the ranch. Zain approached her and Tyler as soon as they stepped through the front door.

"We've got a lead. Nate pulled all your security camera footage from the outside cameras located around the ranch. A black van was on site yesterday while we were here during the search. A man entered the premises wearing an official Henderson County Sheriff's jacket and hat. We think he hid in the house until all of the officers were gone then went into Eli's bedroom after lights out. The camera footage positioned out back showed him carrying Eli out the window, down a ladder and placing him inside the vehicle. We got a hit on a van in the next county over. The van was seen entering a parking garage at the airport. We have a team getting ready to head out."

Carli didn't even remove her bag from her shoulder. "No cops remember. We were supposed to keep this limited to Nate and you."

"They don't know we're coming. They think we're meeting them at the airstrip at six p.m. We go in early, around noon, surprise them and get Eli back. Trust me. We're good at this."

"Fine, but I'm coming too."

"Only if you do exactly what I tell you." Zain looked at Tyler. "What about you?"

Tyler lifted his pants leg. "Can't. Since I'm being charged for murder, thanks to your cronies, the judge is making me wear an ankle bracelet. Doesn't want me to skip town. But you better keep me posted every step of the way. I want my son brought home safe. Once he's found, I'll deal with you and all your nonsense."

Zain gave her brother a quick nod and they joined the group of deputies assembling on Carli's porch. "Okay, everyone. We've been over the details. Let's find this van and then follow my or Nate's lead. We want to bring little Eli home with no injuries for anyone. Got it?"

They all nodded in unison and headed for their cruisers. Carli stepped onto the porch and started for her brother's truck. Zain touched her arm.

"You're riding with me in the surveillance truck."

Great. Another long stressful car ride with another frustrating man.

Zain checked the video feed from Nate's helmet cam again. Everyone was in position waiting for Zain's signal. A dark van, matching the same description from the night at the covered bridge, sat parked on the third level of the Asheville airport parking garage, facing the open-air half wall. No movement could be seen inside or out. He had his team stationed five hundred feet away providing observation updates.

"No thermal heat detected inside the van," one officer stated over the radio.

"Could be lead-lined," Zain said, then glanced at Carli sitting in his passenger seat.

Her eyes were glued to the monitor screens in the surveillance truck. She barely spoke on the drive over and he didn't know how to talk to her after Tyler's arrest. What words could he possibly say to make her understand his dilemma? He wasn't going to apologize for doing his job.

"Are you sure my nephew won't get harmed in any cross fire?" Carli asked.

The awkward silence between them, broken. Zain adjusted the Kevlar vest he wore. "I can't guarantee anything, but we're going to do everything we can to keep him safe."

A glazed look behind her eyes didn't transfer much confidence in his statement. He didn't have time to convince her. "I'm going to need you to stay here. Whatever happens, do not get out of this truck. Okay? Deputy Judd will take care of any questions you have."

She raised her palms into the air. "I'm not going anywhere."

Zain opened the back door and lifted his radio. "All units move into position."

His colleagues joined him, all wearing full tactical gear and weapons aimed at every side. They had to be prepared for anything. Machine gun fire, bombs, etc. They converged around the van, making sure to take cover behind other vehicles.

"Police. Out of the van. Hands up," Nate yelled from his position next to Zain.

No doors opened. Not even a semblance of movement.

A glimmer of metal flashed from the building roof across the airport driveway. Dale oversaw the sniper teams stationed there. Zain hit the talk key on his radio. "Unit 1, do you see any movement from your vantage point?"

Dale's voice rattled through the radio. "All clear." Zain glanced at Nate. "You got my back?"

"Always."

They moved together, like their former days as partners. One of the best teams in the department according to the medals they'd received. Five hundred and forty arrests on their record with the highest percentage of the criminals behind bars.

Nate reached the back door first and held up his hand, signaling to enter. Zain breached the metal door and Nate aimed his gun inside.

The van was empty.

Zain holstered his weapon and climbed into the vehicle. "Clear."

Usually the word brought relief, but not this time. Eli was still out there being held hostage by some lunatic. Zain moved to the front and checked for anything to help him determine Eli's location. This was definitely the right van. A booster seat perfect for a five-year-old sat on the floor.

Funny. Zain had never known any kidnapper to care enough about their captive to make sure they were safe in a vehicle. Most criminals willing to put a kid's life at risk couldn't care less about child seat laws.

He hopped back onto the pavement and placed a hand on Nate's shoulder. "Get a team in here. We need a full sweep. Maybe we'll come up with fingerprints, a hair or something to help us find them."

Nate motioned for his team and began to secure crime scene tape around a designated area. "Will do."

"I'm going to head back to the surveillance truck and update Carli. She can't see anything from here except for what's displayed on the monitors."

"Prayers up, man. Not finding Eli is going to cause more tension between the two of you."

Zain helped secure the tape. "Yeah. She didn't say a word the entire ride here. I guess arresting Tyler has been too much for her. If only she knew I tried to stop Dale."

"When we showed up with the warrant, you

should've seen the look in her eyes when Dale put Tyler in the car. I'm surprised I'm not dead right now."

"Thanks for taking care of her. I know it was a difficult situation and I wanted to be there, but…" Zain pointed to his leg.

"How's the healing process?"

"Better. I'm definitely going to have some scars though. Wearing shorts in the summer will not be pretty."

Nate laughed. "By the way, did you get my email today?"

"I've not even had time to turn on my computer. What was it about?"

"We tracked the prescription numbers on the bottles you found in Sadie's PO box and traced the financials from those sales to someone on the board of a charity called the Sunshine Kids."

"The Sunshine Kids? Never heard of them. What did you find out?"

Nate looked past him and nodded. "I'll tell ya later. You better go take care of her."

Zain turned and Carli was at the far end of the parking garage about one hundred yards away walking toward the scene. He moved in her direction, not wanting any perimeter breaches. Safety was his first priority.

Her tense body language spoke volumes. Zain

stopped a few feet short, giving her enough space to feel comfortable.

"The van was empty. Eli's not here."

Mascara tears streaked her face and she pressed her fingers against her lips. Chipped paint covered only half of each bitten nail. "What now?"

"We go back to your house and wait for another—"

A loud boom vibrated the floor of the parking garage. An unseen force pressed Zain into Carli and they fell to the concrete. Intense ringing deafened any noise around him. His movements slowed and vision blurred. Zain rolled to his back and glanced at Carli. She sat up. No blood or bruises, but dazed.

Multiple car alarms gained volume as his exploding tinnitus faded. Zain scanned the faraway distance. A large hole displayed in front of the van's fiery skeleton. Jagged concrete above opened to blue sky swirled with the haze of black smoke. The parking structure still intact.

Two of his men were down.

Nate was one of them. Deputy Harris the other.

Zain struggled to a standing position and rushed to his friend's side. Nate was unconscious, unmoving. A group of officers huddled around the two of them.

Dale knelt in front of Zain and pressed his radio key. "Officers down. I repeat. Officers down. Explosion in the deck. Asheville Airport. We need an ambulance immediately. Send an ATF team and backup."

Zain placed two fingers to Nate's neck. His pulse was weak. Still breathing. No coughing or external bleeding. No signs of internal damage. Some burns to his legs. Sirens swelled as first responders grew closer. Less than five minutes. Must've been close.

"Hang in there, bud. Help's on the way."

He glanced over at another cop assessing Harris. "How's he?"

The man shook his head, removed his jacket and covered the man's body.

Red and blue lights swirled around Carli. Her injuries were nothing more than a slight headache. Nate and Deputy Harris, however, were not as fortunate.

Paramedics shoved Nate into the back of an ambulance and sped past, sirens blaring. A black bag now held the body of Deputy Harris. The medical examiner's team zipped him up and placed him inside the coroner's van. How many more people had to die before they caught Sadie's killer? And how could anyone think her brother could be the one responsible for the rising death toll?

Zain walked toward her as she sat in the driver's seat of the surveillance truck with the door open, window down.

He looked exhausted, defeated. A pang of empathy squeezed her chest, but she pushed any understanding aside. Her brother sat at home with an ankle bracelet on his leg, worried sick about his son. He should be here trying to find Eli, not concerned with going to prison for a murder he didn't commit. The real killer was still on the loose and Eli was nowhere to be found.

Zain gripped the base of the window. His fingertips black from the soot on Nate's body "I'm going to be several more hours here. I've asked Deputy Judd to take you home. He'll be stationed there all night."

Carli dug her thumbnails into the cushioned rubber covering the steering wheel. "Fine."

He exhaled. "In light of today's events, Eli's kidnapping, and the fact that your brother is on house arrest, the feds are dropping the charges against Tyler. By tomorrow, he'll be a free man again."

She looked at him for the first time since they arrived. Finally. "He should've been a free man this entire time."

"True. I wish I could figure out who's connected enough to kill Sadie, kidnap Eli and blow up vans."

"I might know." Carli hesitated to show him the latest text she'd received, but she needed his help to save her nephew's life. She handed him her phone with an unlocked text displayed. "They sent me this after the explosion."

We told you no cops. We were watching you. One more chance. Tomorrow. 6:00 p.m. Warehouse 7 at the airport.

Zain squeezed his eyes closed. The muscles in his jaw flinched. "All this was a setup?"

Carli took back her phone. "Looks that way. We can't have a large team like this when we go to the warehouse, Zain. Someone on the inside is letting them know our moves. They'll kill Eli and I'll never forgive myself if anything happens to him. They've given us one more chance. We can't blow it."

"My guys are good cops. They'd never betray our operations."

Deputy Judd's car stopped in front of them and the officer stayed in the vehicle.

Carli opened the door, letting her hand rest on Zain's. "Funny, because I don't trust any of them, except for you. And that's pretty insane after all you've put my family through. We've got to do this alone. You and me. Tomorrow, we'll go to the warehouse to get Eli. No one else. Okay?"

Zain pressed his lips together and hesitated. She couldn't risk another catastrophe like this one. "If you don't agree, then I'll text the kidnapper and tell them to set up an earlier time. I'll go alone. Are you with me or not?"

He lifted his gaze to hers, his expression relaxed. "I'm with you. Always have been. Always will be."

FOURTEEN

Zain rested his head against his hands and tried to envision tomorrow's plan one more time. He'd studied the layout of the airstrip and every warehouse on the premises. *Don't skip anything. Walk through each step. Every scripted word Carli has to say.*

His mind kept drifting to her theory. Someone in his department was working with the criminals, feeding them information on every move. But who?

A knock at his door pulled him back to a messy office, a cold cup of coffee on his desk and his lieutenant standing in front of him. "I saw your light. Usually, I'm the last one to leave. You need to go home, Zain. It's after ten. Get some rest."

"I doubt there will be any sleeping tonight, sir. I can't get my mind off Nate. They admitted him to the hospital, and I went by there, but they won't let anyone see him except family. I want an update. I need to know he's going to be okay."

Lieutenant Black took a seat across from him. "He's awake and talking, but still showing signs of a concussion—headache, nausea, etcetera. They moved him from the ICU into a regular observation room. The Kevlar vest he wore protected the rest of his body from the worst of the blast. They won't let anyone see him because he needs to rest and not try to entertain all his visitors. Give him a couple of days and he'll be good as new."

Zain rubbed his hands over his face. Exhaustion had definitely set into his bones. "I keep going back over everything from today and honestly, I don't know how to move forward or how to find Eli. Search teams have scoured the town and Carli's land. No sign of the boy. I'm afraid we're dealing with someone far more sophisticated and smarter than a local thug."

"How *are* Carli and her brother?"

"Distraught. I had Deputy Judd take her home to try to give her some time to rest."

Zain fought the urge to tell him about the new meeting time, tomorrow night at 6:00 p.m. The last thing he wanted was to get Eli hurt.

"Where were you when the explosion happened?"

"Nate and I had finished checking out the van

and found the booster seat. I told Nate to call in an evidence team to sweep the vehicle. Nate asked me if I got his email and then Carli showed up. I didn't want her getting near the scene so I walked off to meet her for an update. Then everything went kaboom."

His lieutenant tapped his fingers together. "How'd they know we were going to be there?"

Zain sat up straighter. "Wait… Nate sent me an email about the Sunshine Kids Charity."

He began to click through the multiple pages of evidence he had open on his screen.

"What's the Sunshine Kids Charity?"

"It's a foundation that raises money to help children diagnosed with cancer. Nate said he traced the prescription bottles to someone on the foundation's board."

Nate's email sat at the top in bold. Zain clicked it open.

Lieutenant Black leaned forward. "Well, what's the message say?"

Nerves tingled as Zain read the documentation aloud. "No wonder they wanted Nate dead. He'd uncovered something much larger than a small-town dealer. Instead, Nate's investigation uncovered a network of fake charities across the nation specializing in distributing opioids with the majority of funds going to the founder of the charity."

Lieutenant Black stepped around the desk to view his screens. "Did he give you a name?"

"Yeah. Why am I not surprised? Dr. Candyce Frye."

Carli sipped her coffee and stared out at the acres of pastureland her parents had given her and Tyler. Reds, golds and the colors of orange dotted the mountains rising behind the fields abutting Crystal Creek. The edge of their property ran along the water's banks. Usually, the autumn scenario brought comfort and peace.

But not this morning.

She was still living the nightmare that plagued her dreams every time she closed her eyes.

Eli was out there somewhere. Perhaps even alone, scared. She feared she might never see her nephew again or he'd be one of those kids on posters no one noticed.

She closed her eyes, and pulled her knees to her chest. *God protect him. Let his captors take care of him and treat him with kindness. Bring him home to us.*

A steady peace washed through her and she lifted her chin to the warm sun beaming onto the porch.

The screen door eased open with a creak. Marta stepped outside with a couple of muffins on a plate.

"Mind if I join you?"

Carli scooted over and patted the cushion covering the large bench seat of the swing her father had made. His hand-carved boards still held the designs she'd loved to trace with her fingers as a child. "Please, come sit for a while."

Dark circles rimmed the underside of Marta's eyes. Her usual smiling face turned down. She let her tears fall without swiping them away.

"The house seems empty now. I'm used to Eli bounding down the stairs in the morning, ready to gobble up anything I fix. Those red curls in a mess, all over his head. Now there's nothing but the gurgle of the coffeepot."

Carli took her hand. "At least we know the captors are holding Eli somewhere and he's not wandering the fields or property alone. They know he's their leverage to get the evidence and money from me. They won't hurt him or we won't give them what we have."

"Monsters. Anyone who takes a child from his bed is nothing but a monster."

Carli brushed away another falling tear from her cheek. "I wish I could hear his little voice one more time or see those cute freckles all bunched up on his nose when he grins."

Marta squeezed her hand. "Not knowing the location of someone you love is the toughest thing anyone can go through. Questions arise.

Are they safe, hurt or cold? The absence becomes a living nightmare, repeating every day until they're found."

Something in Marta's tone of voice reflected more than their current situation. The woman never talked about her past, but something in her words signified she was reliving a previous trauma. "Did you lose someone you loved?"

Marta's foot braked the motion of the porch swing, her demeanor serious. She fidgeted with the loose threads from a frayed cushion edge. A slight breeze tossed wisps of dark hair streaked with silver from her friend's face. A simple beauty lived in Marta's high cheekbones and full lips. Her eyes lifted. Green like Carli's.

"I lost you."

Carli didn't understand. Marta had always been in her life, taking care of many details every day. "You haven't lost me, Marta. I'm always here for you. Just because I moved to Atlanta doesn't mean you lost me."

She placed her reassuring hand on top of Marta's while the woman shook her head.

"That's not what I mean. I've waited a long time to tell you this because there never seemed to be a right time, and I'm not sure now is the right time either, but I can't wait any longer."

Carli set her mug on the porch floor and took both of Marta's hands in hers as a source of encouragement. "You can tell me anything, Marta. Go ahead. Don't be afraid."

The woman's face paled. "I'm your biological mother."

The four words punched the air from Carli's lungs. Her mind whirled trying to make sense of the unexpected statement. Never did she dream the woman who had taken care of her all these years was her real mother. Her parents never alluded to that truth. How could they keep something this important from her?

"Carli? Did you hear what I said?"

She stood on weakened legs and crossed to the railing taking in the expansive view. "Yeah. I heard."

Her fingers gripped the painted wood, its strength holding her upright.

Marta was her mother.

They didn't even look much alike. Marta had dark hair with a plump stature. Not the DNA for a tall, pale redheaded woman. Maybe she took after her dad. Carli faced her again.

"Who's my father?"

Marta's gaze dropped to her lap where a lone string on her apron claimed her attention. "He was a ranch hand who worked weekends for your father. I loved him and we got married on the covered bridge with Crystal Creek running beneath us. We were married for two years. Those were the happiest days of my life."

A small smile curled the corners of Marta's lips with the memory, but as quickly as it came the joy faded. "But he had a dark past and evil followed him here. One night, some men he owed money to found him outside of town and took his life."

Her sad eyes lifted to Carli's transferring the burn of loss into her. "A week later, I found out I was pregnant with you. I had no job, no money and with him gone, I planned to give you up for adoption. The Moores wanted to adopt you. Give you their name. In this town, their family name held a great reputation and would provide you with things I never could. They wanted me to be a part of your life, hired me as your nanny. We planned to tell you when you were older, but as you entwined into their family, I saw how happy you were and didn't want to take that away from you. God provided for us and let me be with you every day. How could I ask Him for more?"

Carli leaned her back against the porch post. She understood the situation. Even loved her parents for helping out a destitute woman. But she struggled to get past the fact that no one ever told her the truth.

"Why didn't you tell me after my parents died?

Two years have gone by and you had every opportunity to speak up and didn't."

Marta stopped picking at the string and clasped her hands together. "I should have, but I was afraid."

Carli folded her arms and tried to contain the rage building within her. "You knew the torment I went through after they died and when I found out the truth about my adoption, and *you* were afraid? I've wondered about my identity, why my real parents gave me up, the color of my parents' eyes. You had the answers and yet you chose to leave me in the dark. How could you do that? A real mother would never let her child go through that kind of pain without sharing the truth."

Marta kept her wet face downcast, her shoulders shook with sobs.

Any other day, Carli would've wrapped the woman in a hug and offered comfort, but this was all too much to process.

She needed time to think and had to get out of there.

This was too hard.

Time to leave.

A protective trait she'd mastered over the years.

With two strides, Carli stepped from the porch, hopped in the ATV and headed to the old barn. Cocoa stamped his feet when she entered. He was the only living creature in her life who was loyal and faithful.

The only friend she could trust.

Zain picked up Dale and headed to town. "It all makes sense now. Candyce was creating fake charts from deceased patients and prescribing opioids in regular quantities to remain under the radar. She then sold them on the black market to make money and deposited said money into the Sunshine Kids Charity fund. Then she'd transfer the money into two offshore accounts in the Cayman Islands."

"And Nate sent all this to you in an email?"

"Pretty much. Sadie must've caught on to her scheme while she was working in Dr. Frye's office and planned to expose her. After she killed Sadie, she even used my sister's name to prescribe more pills."

"What about the photo and blood evidence of Sadie being at the drug bust? How do you explain away those facts?"

"Candyce told me she used to have Sadie deliver drugs to their patients. The team found a former patient who used to live in the same house before the drug bust. The video date and time stamp had been doctored."

"And the blood?"

"Sadie had the in-office lab draw her blood

work for her annual physical. Easy to plant. Anyway, I've got an arrest warrant for Candyce. She should be at her office."

Dale pulled out his Ka-Bar police-issued knife and lightly rubbed his thumb across the serrated blade, then cleaned it with a cloth in his pocket. "Candyce is not a large woman. How do you explain her lifting a sledgehammer to hit Sadie in the barn?"

"She would never get her designer clothes dirty. She hired a hit man. Explains the man who shot Carli. Probably why she had two accounts in the Cayman Islands. One for him and one for her."

Zain pulled into the parking lot of the multiplex office building where Dr. Frye's medical clinic was located. Other patrons from nearby businesses stopped and gawked at the flashing lights. He and Dale moved to the door and went inside.

The place buzzed with activity. Patients sat in almost every chair waiting to be seen. Zain flashed his badge at the receptionist desk and she clicked the internal door open for them to pass through to the nursing area.

Julia Adams stood on the other side of the entrance to welcome them. "Sergeant Wescott? Back so soon? How's Carli doing?"

"She's good."

Julia's blue-eyed gaze focused on Dale. "And who'd you bring with you?"

"This is Agent Hunt with the DEA's office."

"Oh, a fed. How impressive." She extended her hand with a flirty smile. "Nice to meet you."

"Wow. You're stunning."

"Thank you."

Zain didn't have time for this mating game. "Listen, Julia, I need to see Dr. Frye immediately. Official police business."

Her expression straightened and she released Dale's hand. "I wish I could help you, but she took today off. Said she was going away for the weekend and wanted to get an early start." Julia's focus turned back to Dale. "Anything I can help you with?"

"Do you know where she went?" Dale asked.

"She didn't say. Probably a beach somewhere. The woman loves the ocean."

Zain handed Julia a business card. "Why don't you give me a call if she contacts you and keep our visit between us, okay?"

"Sounds good. Have a nice day."

The officers exited the building and climbed into the SUV. Zain hit the steering wheel with his fist.

Dale held up his hands. "Whoa. Don't take it out on the vehicle."

"She bailed."

"Yeah. But that means she's guilty and more than likely has Eli."

Zain inserted his key into the ignition and started the SUV, then glanced over at Dale. "I can't believe you told Julia she was stunning."

Dale responded with a wink. "Just call 'em like I see 'em."

FIFTEEN

Despite being outside, Carli struggled to breathe. She dug her heels into Cocoa's side and raced for the covered bridge.

Wonder if her mother helped Marta with her wedding. Provided the food or decorations. Did they have pictures? Was there a photo of him?

Both her fathers were gone. How scared Marta must've been to lose her husband and find out she was pregnant. Fear consumed Carli's life after her parents were killed. She couldn't imagine if she'd had a baby to raise. Yet her parents stepped up and helped this woman in need. A kind gesture. Her parents allowed Marta to be a large part of her life. She was there at every birthday, Christmas—and helped with the famous Moore family cookouts on New Year's Eve.

They raised her together. Then why was the news so difficult to accept?

Carli pushed Cocoa into a faster gallop across

the pasture and hoped the passing scenery might help make sense of all she'd learned.

The covered bridge came into view and a tightening of the reins slowed Cocoa to a trot. Her horse's hooves clopped across the boards covering Crystal Creek. Carli stared between the slats at the babbling brook underneath and leaned forward, her head resting against Cocoa's neck. Animals seemed to understand her better than anyone.

On the other side, she dismounted and led Cocoa down to the water for a drink.

Carli removed her shoes and stuck her toes into the cold stream. A few more months and ice would form on the edges; her days of riding would be limited once winter hit. She'd have to wait for warmer weather.

Her parents used to bring Tyler and her to the creek in the summers. They'd dam up a swimming hole and let them play for hours. Marta always joined them.

Her whole life Marta took care of her, helped with homework, wiped away her tears when a friend hurt her feelings. She'd grown up with this woman as a part of their family but never dreamed she was a blood relative.

Carli tied off Cocoa to the bridge and meandered up the hill. One large gray stone protruded up from the ground. Her parents' names were inscribed on the front. Could she even call them her parents anymore? The last name MOORE was engraved in the center. But now with Marta as her mother, keeping their last name seemed unfitting.

Leaves crunched behind her and Carli spun around. Tyler stood there, his hands in his pockets. Had he kept this a secret from her too?

"Did you know?" she asked.

He shook his head. "Just found out. Walked into the kitchen and Marta was in tears. Told me everything. You okay?"

Carli turned back to her parents' graves, knelt on the damp ground and began to remove overgrown grass from the stone's edge. "I don't know. I guess I shouldn't have stormed out of the house."

"I think Marta understands. She's been with us for years. If anyone knows you, she does, and I'm sure she understands you need some time to process this news."

"Yeah. Life-altering news."

"Is it really though?"

Carli snatched another clump of grass and threw it to the side. "Uh…yes."

Tyler took a seat on the grass beside her. "You know, I can't imagine what you're going through, but can I say one thing without you getting all defensive?"

"Of course. You're the only person in my life I'd listen to right now."

He picked a couple of blades of grass and let the wind blow them from his hand. "I'd give anything to have my mother again. To hear her laugh. See her smile. Give her a hug. This is like a second chance for you. You have a woman who loves you, a woman who gave birth to you, in your life. That's something I'll never have again."

She leaned against him, tears filling her eyes. "You're right. Marta has always been the strong, Godly woman we've loved all our lives. I just wish she would've told me sooner." She motioned a hand toward her adopted parents' graves. "Or they would've told me."

He squeezed her close and planted a kiss on her head. "Well…you know now. What are you going to do about it?"

Carli stood and dusted off her jeans, then helped Tyler to his feet. "What I should've done a long time ago. Move back to the ranch and get to know my mother."

Tyler wrapped his arms around her and gave her a hug. "You know this doesn't change anything between us. You'll always be my little sister."

"I better be." She gave him an extra squeeze.

"You know Marta, Eli and I will always be your family."

"I know."

He stepped back and lifted the leg of his pants. "Guess who's finally free?"

The ankle bracelet was gone. Zain had kept his word. "Oh, great. When did they come by and remove it?"

"Zain stopped in, apologized, took it off and is waiting for you at the house. Time to go get my son back."

"Then you're coming with us?"

"There's nothing that would keep me from finding Eli and bringing him home."

Darkness covered the sky by six in the evening. Carli longed for daylight saving time and warm summer months. But the fall days had moved into colder nights. At least the lack of light provided cover for their operation.

Carli sat in the truck at the edge of the airstrip and waited for Zain's signal to move into position. Warehouse 7 was at the end of the strip, on the left. Zain and Tyler were parked in an abandoned parking lot down the street out of sight. Both were armed and excellent shots. She was also packing. Not taking any chances when the life of her nephew was at stake.

Zain agreed to keep their team small, finally listening to her. They still didn't know who the inside mole was, so they kept this operation under wraps. Even Dale was kept out of the loop.

Carli's earpiece clicked on.

"Time is six o'clock. Move slow and do exactly as I tell you," Zain said.

She inched the truck forward onto a dirt road beside the warehouses. A Cessna jet sat at the end of the runway. No sign of Candyce.

A black bag sat in Carli's passenger seat holding the prescription bottles and a two-million-dollar check demanded for ransom. Several of the containers had fake pills with microchips implanted inside them to provide tracking capabilities. They'd catch her one way or the other.

Three bright lights from the front of the plane switched on and the engine roared to life. Carli flicked her headlights up a notch also. No harm in brightening up the space like a noonday Western movie. Make the scene more visible for Zain and Tyler as they watched through the mounted camera on the front of the truck.

The door to Warehouse 7 opened.

Dressed in an all-black outfit, a woman emerged and walked toward the jet.

No designer heels.

No fancy clothes.

They'd made a mistake.

Dr. Candyce Frye wasn't the one who took Eli.

Instead, a woman with a blond ponytail turned her face and looked directly into Carli's gaze.

Julia Adams.

"Zain, are you seeing this?"

"Is that Dr. Frye's nurse?"

"In the flesh."

Carli couldn't break her gaze from the woman. Julia was supposed to be Sadie's friend and colleague.

How could she do something so horrible?

A large, muscular man followed Julia, but Eli was not with them. Was he in the warehouse?

Julia boarded the plane, while her henchman stood at the bottom of the stairs, armed and ready for any trouble.

"What is she doing, Zain? I thought she wanted her money and merchandise."

"Give her a minute. She'll call your cell. When she does, answer."

He barely finished the statement when her phone rang. Carli hit Accept.

"Glad you wised up this time and came alone."

Carli remained calm although every instinct inside her wanted to ram the truck into the plane's landing gear. "Where's my nephew, Julia?"

"He's safe and if you do everything I say, he'll remain that way. Now, step from your vehicle with the evidence and your phone, then stand in the middle of the airstrip across from Warehouse 7."

Carli shoved her loaded gun into the back of her pants, lifted the bag and stepped outside, Zain still in her ear. "Go slow. No sudden movements. Mission is to bring Eli home safe even if Julia escapes."

Carli didn't respond to his statement. This woman wasn't getting away, not on her watch. Julia had to pay for all she'd done to her family behind the guise of a respected reputation. Carli put the phone on speaker and tucked it into her shirt pocket to free her hands.

"I can't believe you pulled this off right underneath Dr. Frye's nose."

"Pretty easy, really. Candyce was always so enamored with Sadie, that I could do about anything without her knowing. The benefit of being invisible. Now place the bag on the ground and step back ten steps."

Carli tossed the bag onto the ground with a thud. "Did you kill her? Did you kill Sadie?"

Zain didn't like her question. "Carli—stay on script. No questions, remember?"

She ignored his command. "Because I want you to know… If you killed my best friend, no matter what happens tonight, I'll hunt you down until I find you and make you pay for her death."

"Now, now, Carli. Don't be hostile. Of course,

I didn't kill Sadie. She was an amazing coworker, just got a bit nosy."

"You hired someone else to knock her off, is that it? Didn't even have the decency to get your hands dirty?"

Zain remained silent, despite his previous demand. She knew he wanted to know these answers too.

The man in black walked toward Carli, gun raised. "Is this the man you paid to take Sadie's life? Are you going to take mine too?"

He stood right in front of her, unfazed by their conversation. Muscles filled out the black T-shirt he wore, but if the man had any military or law enforcement training, he would've checked Carli for weapons. Might be a killer, but not a smart one.

He knelt to the ground, opened the envelope, tapped an app on his phone and photographed the check. The money was being deposited into a bank account.

This was Carli's chance. His eyes weren't even on her. The man might be muscular, but probably slow. By the time he got to his feet, she could be at the door to the warehouse. Zain and Tyler would back her up and keep her safe.

With one quick motion, Carli sprinted forward, plowed into the man and knocked him on his back. His gun skidded across the dirt. Carli hurdled his straggling grasp and raced to door number seven. She ducked when shots fired, but kept moving. The plane began to accelerate down the runway.

Julia's voice scolded her. "I didn't think you had it in you, Carli. I'm kind of impressed, but you really shouldn't have attacked my employee. Poor Eli. Now I have to pull my trigger."

The call ended.

Carli halted her jog and scanned the perimeter. What did she mean pull her trigger? Adrenaline rushed through her body. She had to get to Eli before Julia hurt him.

Flames ignited on one side of the warehouse building. Images of the barn fire flashed through Carli's mind. "No!"

"Get to the building, Carli. We're coming." Zain's shout pierced her ear, but triggered her legs into a full run. Another burning building. Eli's screams met her ears.

"Help me! Someone help me!"

"Eli!" she screamed. "Get away from the door, I'm going to shoot the lock." With a slight pause and no more screams, Carli fired at the handle and the door opened. Airstrip lighting cast a glow inside the dark room.

Her nephew stood against the wall opposite the door. He looked well kept. Hair brushed and dressed in clean clothes. She started for him, arms out when Eli's eyes widened. "Look out, Aunt Carli!"

A shadow in the door behind her blocked the glow. A strong hand grasped Carli from behind and squeezed, dragging her backward from the building.

She tried to fire a few random shots behind her, but none connected. Her magazine was empty. Zain and Tyler rounded the corner of the building.

They both aimed their weapons at the man, but he placed Carli in front of him. "If you want to keep them both safe, then hold your fire. The girl and I will be leaving."

Carli struggled against him, kicking her feet, clawing his arm. He didn't flinch. Her boots created drag marks in the dirt. They were almost to the end of the warehouse.

Zain and Tyler kept their guns aimed, proceeding forward at a slow pace. Black smoke billowed from Eli's location. They needed to hurry. Save her nephew.

Zain said something to Tyler and walked past the door.

"Get E—" Carli tried to say, but the man squeezed tighter cutting off her statement. He pulled her around the corner to a parked car with tinted windows at the end of the building.

Blackness faded into the edges of her vision.

Carli sucked in a small breath. Oxygen. She needed air.

Fight, Carli. Don't let him get you in the car.

She clamped her teeth onto his arm. He cursed, but didn't loosen his grasp.

A door clicked open behind them and his grip tightened, stifling any movement she could muster.

Another person was behind them. "Good job, Kenta. Now let's get her in the car."

Male voice. Almost recognizable, but Carli couldn't place the identity.

A strong prick stung her neck, injecting pain. Drugs. Probably a gift from Julia. Haziness disturbed her vision. She'd been here before. The night of the party.

Fight abandoned her body. Every scene around her lagged like a bad connection and she struggled to awaken her brain. *Don't go to sleep. Don't go to sleep.*

The other person moved. Another car door opened and closed. She tried to see the second man's face, but Kenta held her firm.

Zain rounded the corner. Blurry arm raised.

Get Eli, Zain. Leave me. Get Eli.

No words emerged from her lips. Instead, Kenta tossed her into the back seat of the car and slammed the door. Shots fired.

The vehicle lurched tossing Carli onto the

floor behind the passenger seat. She grasped the console to steady herself and glanced up at the driver. His face blurred, but something was familiar about him.

"Hello, Carli."

His greeting was cordial, as if they were friends. If only her brain could think. The drugs were in full effect now. She collapsed back into the seat. Blackness engulfed her consciousness. The scent of cinnamon lingered in the air.

SIXTEEN

Zain dove behind a large cylinder container to dodge the rounds of ammo aimed in his direction. He peered around the edge and fired a few more shots at the large man, who the driver called Kenta. Zain followed him to another large warehouse building farther down than the one burning.

Carli's life depended on Kenta's capture. They couldn't let this criminal escape. He was the only one who knew where the driver took Carli.

Zain tried to get a look at the man in the car, but the windows were too dark. Carli would be miles away by the time he found Kenta. He pressed his back against the side of the building. Footsteps slapped the concrete inside and faded into the shadows of the warehouse. He signaled for Tyler to run with Eli to the other end of the building. At least the boy was safe, but Zain was on his own. He'd have to take down this monster alone.

With one swift motion, Zain released the empty clip and reloaded a new magazine. He raced to the side of the occupied building and crept along the side wall to the entrance.

Zain peered inside. Dark, dusty with tall racks filled with airplane parts and other mechanical equipment. A variety of places to hide. Drops of fresh blood dotted the floor. Confirmation Zain's shot hadn't missed.

At least Kenta's loss of blood would weaken any attacks. As long as Zain stayed out of his line of fire.

He crept through each aisle clearing it of danger. Only one more to go. Zain rounded the corner, weapon aimed and ready for a fight.

A strong hand grabbed his leg.

"Help me," Kenta whispered from his propped-up position against a shelf. His skin dripped with sweat. The man slid his gun across the floor and held up his wrist. Zain slapped on the cuffs, then called for an ambulance.

"What's your full name?"

"Kenta Lucas."

His eyes were losing focus, but he fumbled a hand inside his jacket.

Zain placed his foot on his wrist and stopped him. He might have another weapon. "Hold up. I'll get it."

Kenta's body went limp. He'd lost consciousness. Sirens blared in the distance. Zain knelt closer. His hand brushed the blood-drenched shirt and pulled something hard from his pocket.

He flipped over the object.

Kenta was a DEA agent.

The man released an audible breath. Zain checked his pulse. His skin was clammy.

Kenta was barely alive.

Back at the office, Zain shuffled through file after file, looking for anything to help him locate Carli before it was too late. Kenta's information included a stint in the military where he was honorably discharged and a mediocre career as a DEA agent. Nothing much to help him find Carli.

Tyler rushed in without an invitation, Eli still in his arms. His face was red either from running through the parking lot or from anger at how the sting went down. "How are we going to find her now? I can't believe you let them take her."

Zain held up a palm to stop him. More stress and negativity were not what he wanted to hear. He berated himself enough for the entire sheriff's department.

"I didn't let anyone take her. They escaped before I could get past Kenta. And now he's unconscious in the ICU."

"Well, what are we going to do? We have to find my sister before they hurt her."

Zain needed to think and although he understood Tyler's concern, he had to figure this out alone. "*We* aren't going to do anything. I, however, will handle this with my team. You should take Eli home."

The boy looked healthy in his father's arms despite the tear-stained smudges of dirt on his face. Julia had provided quality care for Eli while she kept him in captivity. Paramedics at the scene said not a curl on his head was harmed in any way.

Zain hoped Eli was young enough to forget the entire ordeal, but at five years old a few emotional scars were bound to linger from the extent of his abduction.

Eli lifted his head and put his hands on his father's cheeks. "I want to go home, Daddy. Go find Aunt Carli there."

Tyler's face softened at his son's request. He glanced at Zain. "I want to know what's happening at all times. Keep me in the loop on this, Sergeant, and bring her home."

Zain gave him a nod as he left, then searched for Deputy Judd's number. Zain had stationed him outside the ICU door, monitoring everyone who accessed the medical space as well as keeping tabs on Kenta's progress.

Julia, on the other hand, was long gone. Took off in her Cessna with her money to an undisclosed location.

Kenta was the only one who knew the identity of the driver in the car. When the criminal woke up, he wanted to be the first to question him. Carli's life depended on his knowledge unless Zain found another way.

His officer answered on the first ring. "Judd here."

"Any change?"

"No, but I'll let you know as soon as his condition improves."

"Any visitors?"

"Not a one."

"Okay... Thanks."

He ended the call and closed his eyes, trying to force his brain to come up with a plan to find Carli. Coffee might help.

Zain made his way to the lounge area and found a fresh pot of black brew. Nate's name flashed across his phone. Zain picked up.

"I hear you got discharged."

"Yeah. Looks like I'll be stuck at home for the next couple of days."

"I'm so glad you're okay."

Nate cleared his throat. "Now, don't go getting all sentimental on me. I called about Carli.

I heard about the airstrip. Did they really take her?"

Zain leaned against the counter and shook a sugar packet in his hand. "I lost her, Nate. I was on him, thought I could get to her, then the next thing I know, she's shoved into a car and the guy shot at me. The car's gone and the only witness I've got who can give me any information is lying in the ICU, unconscious. I knew this was a bad idea."

"What about the trackers we planted?"

"Still in the black bag that apparently no one cared enough to take with them. Kenta chased Carli and left the bag sitting on the ground right where Carli tossed it. The evidence was just a distraction for Julia to get her money and leave."

"Then maybe I've got some news that can help."

"I'm listening."

"When I heard about what happened at the airstrip, I decided to poke around a bit for you. Kenta's effects were cataloged in the database. I pulled everything up on my laptop and found something interesting. Do you remember when Carli's tire got slashed at the coffee shop?"

Zain poured the sugar into the black liquid and stirred the contents. "Yeah. Seems like she's had that happen several times."

Zain's phone dinged with a text message.

"I just sent the images over to you. Notice anything about the cut?"

Zain leaned in for a closer view. "Looks serrated, with a wide base."

"Exactly. I think this is a Ka-Bar TDI knife."

"The ones issued to law enforcement?"

"Yeah."

"I don't know. That's a tough sell with the number of serrated knives out there." Zain slid his knife from his belt and compared the markings. "Besides, ours aren't serrated."

"Nope. But the DEA gives their agents ones that are. I did a little experiment and matched Kenta's DEA blade to the image of Carli's tire marks. They were the same."

"So, Kenta slashed her tire?"

"Not exactly. That was my first thought too. Makes sense, right? But anybody can get their hands on one of these knives."

Zain took a sip of his coffee and tried to follow Nate's thought process. "I guess I'm confused."

"I tracked Kenta's location and he was three thousand miles away on the day Carli's tire was slashed. I got Heather to send me her security camera footage outside her shop on the same day. You'll never believe who I saw."

Another ding. Nate had messaged a video clip for Zain to view.

"There was only one other DEA agent in town with a Ka-Bar serrated knife."

The sweetness of Zain's coffee turned in his stomach as he stared at the image of his longtime friend.

"Dale's the killer."

Carli's head pounded. Not like a simple headache from lack of caffeine. The pain was consuming. She rolled onto her side. A cold, hard surface beneath her.

Darkness surrounded her with a dim light coming from another area. Where was she? Her hands were duct-taped together in front of her. She pressed up to a sitting position. Water babbled nearby and the musty smell reminded her of only one place.

The cavern where Sadie's body was found.

A low mumble reached her ears from the outer chamber. Carli curled her feet underneath her and stood, leaning against the rock wall. She massaged the throb pulsating her temples, but the torment continued. If she was going to make it out of this alive, then she needed to free her hands.

She raised her arms over her head and dropped them straight down. The tape loosened. She tried again, ripping her constraint in half.

A shadow stepped into the doorway. Light

from the outside chimney highlighted the man's body from behind.

"Well, I see you finally came to."

His voice triggered a recollection. Memories of the night Sadie died rushed back like a tsunami.

The glow of a battery-powered lantern exposed his identity when he stepped into view.

Dale Hunt had been in the car with Sadie. She'd let him out at the old barn, before heading on up the hill to meet Tyler at the road.

She remembered.

"You killed her."

After he moved a couple of steps closer, he positioned the lantern in the middle of the room. "Not on purpose. But she discovered too many of my secrets and planned to go to the cops. I couldn't let that happen."

"And now I know your secrets. I'll make sure you rot in jail."

Dale skulked closer and Carli backed against the wall. He reached out and let his fingers touch her cheek. "I don't think so. You're going to be long gone before anyone finds you. Maybe I'll even dump your body over the same cliff where your parents died. You should've heard their screams as I pushed them over the edge. Sad, really. I always liked your father."

Adrenaline rushed through every muscle in her body. "You killed them?"

He shrugged his shoulders. A dismissal of their lives with a simple gesture. "Yeah. You'd be surprised how easy it is to doctor police reports when you have federal access."

"If you liked my father, then why did you kill them?"

"They found some of the drugs in Sadie's bag one evening when she was at your home. She told them everything she'd discovered about Julia. I couldn't let Sadie rat out the woman and the money I love."

He leaned in and let his fingers move down the side of her neck, while his gaze skimmed lower. "One thing's for sure. You are a beautiful woman. Too bad I'm going to have to kill you."

Carli flinched and inched toward the exit. Keep him talking and she might be able to escape. "So, you killed my parents and my sister-in-law and then you killed Sadie in my old barn the night of the party."

"I really don't want to talk about them. They're gone. Been dead for years now. I'm sure we can find something more interesting to discuss. Aren't you?"

Disgust coiled inside of Carli. All the pieces she tried to figure out, connected before her like a finished jigsaw puzzle. "And after you killed her, you moved her here."

"I couldn't let Zain find her on my property."

He approached her again and Carli inched closer to the cave exit. He managed to remain between her and the door. Dale removed his gun from his holster and checked the magazine. "Thing is, Carli, I always had a crush on you. Wondered what it might be like to have you all to myself. Planned to find out the night of the party, but Sadie rescued you too quick. Never did I think I might get a chance like that again."

His eyes locked with hers. A darkness behind his gaze.

Dale grabbed her arm, pressed the gun to her head and shoved her against the rock wall. "You're going to do everything I say."

This was the moment when she could fight and flee or be killed. She lunged for the exit.

Dale caught her braid from behind and jerked her back. His arm noosed around her neck. She dug her fingernails into his skin, drawing blood.

"You're a lot like her. Sadie fought hard too."

Zain combed through all the files he could find on Dale and even contacted his agency. The DEA thought he was working an undercover sting.

Zain slapped another paper file closed. "I can't

find anything to give me a hint of where Dale would take Carli. No family cabins, favorite vacation spots, and no real estate other than his apartment in Asheville. The team I sent there found no sign of him."

Zain's phone vibrated. He didn't recognize the number, but answered anyway. Maybe someone on the tip line they'd set up had panned out a lead.

"Hi, Zain. This is Marta. Eli might know where they took Carli."

Zain stood, grabbed his keys and motioned for Nate to follow him. "And?"

"He drew a picture of a cave."

SEVENTEEN

Zain and Nate bounded onto the porch steps and Marta met them at the door.

"Thanks for coming. Eli's in the living room with his father."

Tyler glanced in their direction when they entered the room. "He had a nightmare about the fire and Carli. He's cried and clung to me ever since. Said Julia told him to keep quiet or she'd hurt Carli. We couldn't get much more out of him."

God, please protect her. Show me where she is.

Zain placed a hand on the little boy's back and rubbed circles. "Hey, Eli. Remember me? Sergeant Wescott? We're here now and we're going to keep you safe. Nothing to be afraid of."

The boy's sobs softened and he sat up in his father's arms. "But you didn't keep Aunt Carli safe."

Kids. They were honest. Had to give the boy props. "Good point. And that's why I brought along Detective Nate. He's stronger and smarter than me, plus he fights off bad guys all the time."

Eli put his index finger in his mouth. "Then maybe you should send him to get Aunt Carli out of the cave."

Zain straightened at the boy's comment. "Why do you think Carli's in the cave?"

"Ms. Julia told them to take her there. To the cave."

Zain turned to Nate, pulled him onto the porch and unholstered his weapon. "Stay here with them. I don't want Dale escaping and circling back to torment this family anymore. I'll go check the cave and see if what Eli says is true. Radio for backup just in case."

"Be careful, man."

Zain took two strides off the porch and climbed into the SUV. His headlights bumped across the ruts in the road from a recent rainstorm and he veered from the gravel onto pastureland. He'd cut around to the other side of the cave and come in from the back to keep Dale from expecting anything.

A few more curves and his lights reflected off black metal. The same car he saw Carli get pushed into at the airstrip was parked behind a grove of trees adjacent to the cave. The vehicle was positioned for an easy getaway, but Zain blocked the exit with his SUV then edged his way to the cave entrance.

Dale's voice echoed from within. "I promise

I'll make it quick, painless. Don't worry. Jesus will be on the other side. At least that's what Sadie always said."

Fury flooded every inch of Zain, but he had to remain calm, levelheaded. Sadie deserved her killer behind bars. Carli deserved to live.

"I guess when you pushed my family over the cliff, you didn't care about their pain, did you?"

Zain leaned closer. Dale had killed Carli's parents.

A shuffle of feet scraped across the rock floor. "I made sure they died on impact. Quick."

Keeping close to the wall, Zain slipped in behind Dale and Carli and remained camouflaged in the darkness.

Zain needed a better angle. If he shot, he risked hitting Carli, but if he didn't Dale was bound to take her life.

"You are a clever one, Carli Moore. I never expected you to figure all this out. Especially before Zain. He's usually more on top of his game. Didn't even know what was going on right under his nose."

Zain fought the urge to take him out, when Dale stepped within inches of Carli and let his gaze sweep her body.

"You *are* gorgeous, but I never expected a brain in that pretty little head of yours. Quite a surprise. Such a shame you have to die tonight and we couldn't have explored more together."

Enough. Zain straightened and stepped from the shadows, weapon aimed at Dale's head. "Let her go."

Dale grabbed Carli by her braid and pivoted around, placing her between the two of them. He used her as a human shield. At least Zain could look Carli in the eyes now. No fear lived there, just determination.

Dale pressed the Glock to her temple, pulling her head back. Zain kept his gaze focused on her.

A steady strength resonated back to him. Her hands clenched into fists. Zain would get her out of this one way or the other. He refused to lose another person he loved.

Dale smirked. "You came to watch me kill her? A bit morbid, don't you think?"

Zain took a couple of steps closer. "You're not going to kill anyone. Time to turn yourself in."

"Not an option."

Zain took another step forward. "This is over, Dale. Don't do anything to make this worse. We can work something out. A lesser sentence. No lawman wants to spend time in prison with the same men he placed there."

If Zain could keep the man talking, then he wasn't shooting anyone. Dale understood police tactics. Zain had to think outside of the box. Surprise him.

"Too late, my friend. I've got a bank account in the Cayman Islands with enough money to keep me set for life. Thanks to Julia."

"You mean the woman who left you behind and took all the money for herself?"

Dale's eyes blinked a couple of times. "She's waiting for me. Getting everything ready."

"And you both were in this together?"

"Like I'd tell you. A man's gotta keep some of his plans to himself."

Zain kept his eyes on Carli. He needed to move closer for a better shot. If only she could shift to the side a little.

Dale loosened his hold on Carli's braid and pushed her forward. The gun was still aimed at her head. "I think it's time we end this little game."

With one swift motion, Carli dropped with all her weight, turned and struck the barrel of the gun pushing it toward Dale's head as he pulled the trigger. A shot fired. The two of them fell to the ground.

Zain stumbled toward them. "Carli!"

He rushed over and gathered her in his arms. "Carli. Talk to me."

Her whole body shook and she grasped his

arms, her eyes darting around frantic. Zain scanned her for any wounds. There were none.

Her body was injury free.

She glanced at her lifeless abductor. "Is he dead?"

Zain helped her stand to her feet and then checked Dale for a pulse. No heartbeat.

"He's gone."

She moved into Zain's arms. He twisted the bottom of her braid in his fingers and placed a kiss on her forehead. "It's all over now."

"Eli? What about Eli?"

"He's safe, but worried about you. He's the reason I checked the cave."

"How'd he know?"

"Overheard Julia tell Dale to bring you here." Zain held her tighter. "I don't know what I would've done had something happened to you."

Carli stepped back and glanced at Dale's body one more time. "I'm ready to go."

Officers filed into the cave and began the long and tedious process of working a crime scene. Zain let Nate and his team take care of the details. His focus was Carli. She sat on the tailgate of one of the first responder trucks, being treated according to procedure. Maybe they could take some time away. Go back to Atlanta and move her home.

He couldn't take his eyes off her. Breathtaking.

They'd wasted too much time apart because of Sadie's disappearance and death. No more. Life was to be lived and the only person he wanted by his side every day was the woman in front of him.

She'd accepted him, challenged him, made him a better man. He was stronger now and had hope for the future.

Carli's faith was the reason Zain saw no fear in her eyes when a murderer held her in his grasp. Sadie's killer was no longer a threat. Even Julia had been arrested at her favorite Cayman resort. All because Carli trusted God and He didn't forsake her. Zain wanted that same steady strength in his own life. If God would forgive him after all his failures.

Carli talked to one of his detectives with a blood pressure cuff around her arm. Another medic took all her vital signs, asked her some questions and then released her.

She flashed a smile at him from a distance. A beautiful sight bathed in the depth of their trauma. They weren't the same people they were two years ago and he hoped she was ready to move forward with him.

"Need a ride back to your house?" Zain asked, when he walked up.

She smeared her hand against the cave dirt on

her face. "I need to wash this off. I don't want Eli to see me like this."

"I can sneak you in the back door."

"I've got a better idea."

He followed her to his SUV. Neither said anything as he drove down the gravel road. He kept the pace slow this time with the windows down, letting cool October air rush in around them.

Carli leaned forward and pointed. "Pull off down this path. Then stop by the tree."

Zain followed her directions, parked and stepped outside the vehicle. She took his hand and led him to the banks of Crystal Creek, then slipped off her boots onto the grass. She waded in with rolled-up pants and rinsed water over her face. "Come on in. The temperatures have been in the eighties this past week and the water's not too cold."

She was lying, but he didn't care. He'd go anywhere with her.

Zain took off his socks and shoes, then waded into the water. He flinched at the chill on his legs, but continued toward her.

She turned in circles underneath the moonlit sky, water rippling around her legs, and caught his hands. Soft. Kind. Connected.

He loved her.

"I'm sorry, Carli. I've made so many mistakes,

committed many sins against you and your family. Can you ever forgive me?"

She pressed against him, searching his eyes, then placed a wet palm to his face. "I already have. God has too. Can you forgive me?"

"There's nothing to forgive."

Her lips met his in a light kiss. All of their regrets and pain faded. Zain never wanted to be parted from her again. No other woman measured up. She was the one God had placed in his life, forever. A gift.

He pulled back. "How about a fresh start?"

A nighttime glow highlighted her surprise at his question. "What do you mean?"

"I want to spend time with you, love you again, committed to God, together."

Carli kissed him again.

"Is that a yes?"

She took both his hands in hers. "I never stopped loving you and I want us to remember this moment for a lifetime."

Carli closed her eyes, long dark lashes against her pink cheeks. "Dear Jesus, we give this relationship to You. Help us to love each other and be kind in our actions. Thank You for our second chance. Amen."

Her green eyes opened and found his. "Together?"

Zain squeezed her hands. "Forever."

* * *

The Christmas season arrived and passed quickly with Carli spending every moment with Zain. Even today, as they rode on the ATV out her gravel drive, she savored every moment.

Zain stopped mid-road and pulled out a black scarf.

"Here put this on over your eyes."

"Why?"

"Because I have a surprise."

The silky fabric whipped through her fingers as she tied the homemade blindfold in place. "There. Happy?"

"You can't see, can you?"

"Not a bit."

Zain drove a bit farther, stopped the ATV and took her hand in his.

"Where are you taking me?" she asked.

"You'll see. It's a surprise."

Gravel crunched under her boots and water rushed off to her left. Scents of food wafted around her, making her tummy grumble.

Zain stopped. "Okay. You ready?"

"I've been ready. What is this New Year's Eve surprise you've got for me? Is it a picnic by the creek?"

His body moved behind hers, leaning close to her ear. "Happy New Year's, Carli Moore."

His fingers slipped the knot of the scarf loose

and his hands rested on her shoulders. Carli opened her eyes.

She stood at the door of their renovated barn and took in the most beautiful sight her heart could've ever imagined.

Long tables basked in candles, and greenery lined the main aisle. Ribbons and flowers decorated every stall door. Pots of chili and cast-iron pans of cornbread sat to her left, ready to be served by their mothers, Marta and Ms. Wescott.

Carli scanned each face in the room. At every seat stood a person from the town of Crystal Creek, honoring her and her brother from underneath a banner labeled Moore Family New Year's Eve Cookout.

Zain had revived her parents' tradition.

Cheers and applause erupted around her as she made her way down the center aisle, greeting everyone, even Candyce Frye.

Upon the good doctor's return from her long weekend, Zain informed her of Julia's betrayal and Dale's murders. Seems the two met when Dale busted Julia during one of his DEA operations. Being a shrewd businesswoman, Julia cut him in on her operation. Dr. Frye knew nothing of her trusted employee's drug dealings. Candyce turned over all the faked medical records and any other evidence on Julia's work computer to put the woman behind bars for life. Carli's parents, Eli's mother and Sadie's deaths were all vindicated.

When Carli reached the end of the row, she turned and faced Zain, who still stood in the doorway, watching her. She lifted a glass from the table and took a sip of sparkling apple cider.

"In a million years, I never would've dreamed any of you would be here for a New Year's Eve party. But my parents, along with my biological mother, Marta, began this tradition in this town because they loved living here and they loved all of you."

Carli swallowed down the sob rising in her throat at the good memories. Her eyes scanned the crowd as she moved back in Zain's direction.

"My brother and I love living here too. That's why I'll be moving back to the Moore family ranch to help run the place, so Tyler can follow some of his dreams he's put on hold for far too long. But before we dive into the delicious food Marta has made, I want to raise a glass to the man I love."

The townspeople followed her lead and she focused her attention on Zain. He stood with his hands in his pockets, a beautiful soul who she would love every day for the rest of her life.

Carli stepped within inches of him, letting her words fade so only he could hear. "Zain Wescott, you're everything this girl next door could ever need. I can't wait to live each day, that God gives us, with you."

She held up her glass. "To Zain Wescott."

The crowd repeated her words with a cheer, then milled about around them, filling their bowls and plates with her family's recipes.

She took a sip of the cider and set her glass on the table, then wrapped her arms around him, letting the fullness of her kiss display her love. More shouts and whoops filled the air.

He pulled back and wrapped her in a hug, whispering in her ear, "I love you, Carli Moore."

"I love you too."

Country music began to play and the party began, but Zain took her hand in his. "I've got one more surprise for you."

Carli waved a hand toward the gathering of the town. "Isn't this enough?"

"Nope."

He pulled her out of the barn, into the cold night air. Glad she wore her warm coat and hat. Zain took her around the side of the barn and pointed toward the ladder leading to an observation deck she and Tyler added to view their entire property.

"Ladies first."

Carli climbed to the top and took a seat on the roof. Zain sat beside her and pulled a radio from his pocket. "Okay. It's time."

He scooted closer and wrapped an arm around her. She snuggled into his embrace and waited.

Nothing happened.

"What are we looking for?"

A chuckle vibrated against her back. "You never have been good at waiting."

"Another endearing quality I'm sure you'll learn to love."

He pressed his lips to her cheek. "I already do."

A whistling noise cut through the sky and burst into a rainbow of colors above them. Purples, blues, golds and reds glittered like stars in the night. The townspeople clapped below them, mesmerized by the display. Carli stood to take in the view.

"Look at all the people who showed up. The entire town is here. I can't believe you did all this."

She turned to face Zain and found him on one knee. He took her hand in his, slipping a diamond on her left ring finger.

"I know we've had our ups and downs, but I'm not good at waiting either. I've always loved you, Carli, and I always will. So many things have happened this year, but all of them brought us back together. Your strength and fiery beauty captivate me. I don't want anyone but you. Will you do me the honor and be my wife?"

Peace washed through her. Another one of God's promises, fulfilled.

Fireworks exploded around them and a midnight kiss sealed her answer.

Yes, to Zain Wescott, forever.

* * * * *

Uncover the truth in
thrilling stories of faith in the
face of crime from Love Inspired Suspense.
Look for six new releases every month,
available wherever
Love Inspired Suspense books
and ebooks are sold.
Find more great reads at
www.LoveInspired.com

Dear Reader,

Thank you so much for reading my debut novel, *Cave of Secrets*. Zain and Carli's story transpired from a brainstorming session with friends. These two characters get into some trouble, but together they discover how to forgive and love again.

In this world, I often hear how God loves us no matter what we do. And while that is true, I often wonder how often we ask a different question, "Do we love God?"

When we truly love God, we try our very best to live our lives for Him, choosing His ways over our own selfish desires. We give up pleasures that cause Him pain and choose the things that bring Him love, hope and joy no matter the difficult circumstances surrounding us. I hope Zain and Carli's story displays this kind of love for God and inspires you to love Him too with every decision made.

I'd love to hear from you. Connect with me via Twitter: @shannon_redmon or visit www.shannonredmon.com.

Blessings,
Shannon Redmon

Get 4 FREE REWARDS!

We'll send you 2 FREE Books plus 2 FREE Mystery Gifts.

Love Inspired books feature uplifting stories where faith helps guide you through life's challenges and discover the promise of a new beginning.

FREE Value Over $20

YES! Please send me 2 FREE Love Inspired Romance novels and my 2 FREE mystery gifts (gifts are worth about $10 retail). After receiving them, if I don't wish to receive any more books, I can return the shipping statement marked "cancel." If I don't cancel, I will receive 6 brand-new novels every month and be billed just $5.24 each for the regular-print edition or $5.99 each for the larger-print edition in the U.S., or $5.74 each for the regular-print edition or $6.24 each for the larger-print edition in Canada. That's a savings of at least 13% off the cover price. It's quite a bargain! Shipping and handling is just 50¢ per book in the U.S. and $1.25 per book in Canada.* I understand that accepting the 2 free books and gifts places me under no obligation to buy anything. I can always return a shipment and cancel at any time. The free books and gifts are mine to keep no matter what I decide.

Choose one: ☐ **Love Inspired Romance Regular-Print** (105/305 IDN GNWC) ☐ **Love Inspired Romance Larger-Print** (122/322 IDN GNWC)

Name (please print)

Address   Apt. #

City   State/Province   Zip/Postal Code

Email: Please check this box ☐ if you would like to receive newsletters and promotional emails from Harlequin Enterprises ULC and its affiliates. You can unsubscribe anytime.

Mail to the Reader Service:
IN U.S.A.: P.O. Box 1341, Buffalo, NY 14240-8531
IN CANADA: P.O. Box 603, Fort Erie, Ontario L2A 5X3

Want to try 2 free books from another series! Call 1-800-873-8635 or visit www.ReaderService.com.

---

*Terms and prices subject to change without notice. Prices do not include sales taxes, which will be charged (if applicable) based on your state or country of residence. Canadian residents will be charged applicable taxes. Offer not valid in Quebec. This offer is limited to one order per household. Books received may not be as shown. Not valid for current subscribers to Love Inspired Romance books. All orders subject to approval. Credit or debit balances in a customer's account(s) may be offset by any other outstanding balance owed by or to the customer. Please allow 4 to 6 weeks for delivery. Offer available while quantities last.

Your Privacy—Your information is being collected by Harlequin Enterprises ULC, operating as Reader Service. For a complete summary of the information we collect, how we use this information and to whom it is disclosed, please visit our privacy notice located at corporate.harlequin.com/privacy-notice. From time to time we may also exchange your personal information with reputable third parties. If you wish to opt out of this sharing of your personal information, please visit readerservice.com/consumerchoice or call 1-800-873-8635. **Notice to California Residents**—Under California law, you have specific rights to control and access your data. For more information on these rights and how to exercise them, visit corporate.harlequin.com/california-privacy.

LI20R2

Get 4 FREE REWARDS!

We'll send you 2 FREE Books <u>plus</u> 2 FREE Mystery Gifts.

Harlequin Heartwarming Larger-Print books will connect you to uplifting stories where the bonds of friendship, family and community unite.

FREE Value Over $20

YES! Please send me 2 FREE Harlequin Heartwarming Larger-Print novels and my 2 FREE mystery gifts (gifts worth about $10 retail). After receiving them, if I don't wish to receive any more books, I can return the shipping statement marked "cancel." If I don't cancel, I will receive 4 brand-new larger-print novels every month and be billed just $5.74 per book in the U.S. or $6.24 per book in Canada. That's a savings of at least 21% off the cover price. It's quite a bargain! Shipping and handling is just 50¢ per book in the U.S. and $1.25 per book in Canada.* I understand that accepting the 2 free books and gifts places me under no obligation to buy anything. I can always return a shipment and cancel at any time. The free books and gifts are mine to keep no matter what I decide.

161/361 HDN GNPZ

Name (please print)		
Address		Apt. #
City	State/Province	Zip/Postal Code

Email: Please check this box ☐ if you would like to receive newsletters and promotional emails from Harlequin Enterprises ULC and its affiliates. You can unsubscribe anytime.

> ### Mail to the **Reader Service:**
> **IN U.S.A.:** P.O. Box 1341, Buffalo, NY 14240-8531
> **IN CANADA:** P.O. Box 603, Fort Erie, Ontario L2A 5X3

Want to try 2 free books from another series! Call 1-800-873-8635 or visit www.ReaderService.com.

HW20R2

THE WESTERN HEARTS COLLECTION!

COWBOYS. RANCHERS. RODEO REBELS.
Here are their charming love stories in one prized Collection:
51 emotional and heart-filled romances that capture the majesty
and rugged beauty of the American West!

YES! Please send me **The Western Hearts Collection** in Larger Print. This collection begins with 3 FREE books and 2 FREE gifts in the first shipment. Along with my 3 free books, I'll also get the next 4 books from The Western Hearts Collection, in LARGER PRINT, which I may either return and owe nothing, or keep for the low price of $5.45 U.S./$6.23 CDN each plus $2.99 U.S./$7.49 CDN for shipping and handling per shipment*. If I decide to continue, about once a month for 8 months I will get 6 or 7 more books but will only need to pay for 4. That means 2 or 3 books in every shipment will be FREE! If I decide to keep the entire collection, I'll have paid for only 32 books because 19 books are FREE! I understand that accepting the 3 free books and gifts places me under no obligation to buy anything. I can always return a shipment and cancel at any time. My free books and gifts are mine to keep no matter what I decide.

☐ 270 HCN 5354   ☐ 470 HCN 5354

Name (please print)

Address   Apt. #

City   State/Province   Zip/Postal Code

Mail to the **Reader Service:**
IN U.S.A.: P.O. Box 1341, Buffalo, N.Y. 14240-8531
IN CANADA: P.O. Box 603, Fort Erie, Ontario L2A 5X3